GUNFIGHTER BREED

GUNFIGHTER BREED

Nelson C. Nye

WHEELER
CHIVERS

This Large Print edition is published by Wheeler Publishing, Waterville, Maine USA and by BBC Audiobooks Ltd, Bath, England.

Published in 2006 in the U.S. by arrangement with Golden West Literary Agency.

Published in 2006 in the U.K. by arrangement with Golden West Literary Agency.

U.S. Softcover 1-59722-169-4 (Western)
U.K. Hardcover 1-4056-3703-X (Chivers Large Print)
U.K. Softcover 1-4056-3704-8 (Camden Large Print)

The text of this Large Print edition is unabridged.
Other aspects of the book may vary from the original edition.

Set in 16 pt. Plantin by Ramona Watson.

Printed in the United States on permanent paper.

British Library Cataloguing-in-Publication Data available

Library of Congress Cataloging-in-Publication Data

Nye, Nelson C. (Nelson Coral), 1907–
    Gunfighter breed / by Nelson C. Nye.
        p. cm. — (Wheeler Publishing large print westerns)
    ISBN 1-59722-169-4 (lg. print : sc : alk. paper)
    1. Large type books. I. Title. II. Series: Wheeler large print western series.
PS3527.Y33G824 2006
    813′.54—dc22   2005030648

For
L. Ernenwein
who has a code and *lives by it!*

1

"Write Your Own Ticket!"

So *this* was Six-Shooter Siding!

Telldane, eying the place from beneath a down-jerked hatbrim, thought it about the sorriest town he had ever seen — and he had seen a considerable many.

He fished out the makings and twisted himself a smoke, his somber glance roving uncharitably.

There was damned little to this place, considering what amount of hell was being raised about it. To hear some of them tell it you'd have thought to find a combination Dodge City, Abilene, San Saba and half a dozen other places all rolled into one. In actual fact there was but a single street, a blistering stretch of floured adobe, with over it the choking dust thick-hung like a lemon fog. The Rock Island's tracks, forging stubbornly west, blocked one end; south of it the desert ran, a dun expanse of thorn-pricked sand, supine beneath the dark crouched shape of Tucumcari Mountain.

A construction camp at "end of steel," it

had not even a makeshift depot. One crude sprawling warehouse of whipped pine planks, a handful of sidings, of rusty equipment; shanties of tar paper, boxcar houses, some tents and a packing-case post office. That was all.

"Not even a jail!" Telldane snorted.

Be wasting his time in a place like this. Be better, he thought, to push on to that old brawling cow town that was three miles north on the banks of the Pajarito. Liberty, at least, would have decent saloons — a rail to rest a man's boot on, plank-walled gambling halls and honky-tonks that would know how to care for a man.

He put his jaundiced stare across the place again and paused, lips pursed in a whistle. A slim girl yonder had stepped out of a shack. A lithe, good-looking girl — *damned* good-looking! Brown hair and brown eyes and a slender shape that was curved just enough, and in just the right places.

Telldane looked her over with interest; and for that one moment their eyes met and locked. With a toss of the head then she slammed to her saddle. He watched her go larruping off through the dust.

When he could see her no longer he shoved back his hat, "Well!" he said, and brushed a hand across his bristly cheeks; and with one eye gone squinted reconsidered the town. "Not so damned bad at that!" he said grinning.

Might be worth his while to stop here after all, he thought. The place was growing. Old Goldenberg, biggest storekeeper in Liberty, was moving over here, they said. And by the look of things — of the street and the walks and the trade going on — more than half of Liberty's sporting crowd was over here already. He eyed the crazy-lettered signs and shrugged with the look of a man to whom little mattered. Afterwards he kneed his roan through the barebacked gang of sweat- and dust-streaked section hands, through the clanging pound of steel on steel — through the bawdy Irish shouting. Crossing the tracks, with the edge of a tune rolled under his tongue he put his bronc down the street.

There was a corral at its farthest corner and, near by, cattle pens were building. Saw rasp and the hammer blows of carpenters mixed up with the grunts and growls of labor made a strange, outlandish sound to a man brought up with cattle. The place was on the move all right.

He left his horse with the corral keeper

and, turning as a man will when he hasn't definite plans, he sauntered back uptown again, with grins for the misspelled legends garishly daubed above the doors. Most of the doors were tow-sack strips that flapped like a hung-out wash.

New and fresh and boisterous was this place called Six-Shooter Siding — new as those planks over there by the tracks, native pine that would curl like a whiplash once the sun got a few hours' work in. New and boisterously proud of itself. Like a half-wit beating a rattle.

And the crowd was boisterous — noisy as hell, with everyone trying to shout down his neighbor, bumping him, prodding him, slapping his back for him. It was all great stuff — if you'd never been anywhere else. But Telldane thought it pretty small beer; he had been plenty other places.

He was passing the land-office tent when it happened. A man came out, flung a look Telldane's way and incontinently dived beneath a hitch rack. He came up crouched and, like a thing on strings, lunged the width of the road, vanishing into an alley. Telldane didn't know him from Adam.

People stared — but not Telldane. This was old stuff; and with a muttered oath he wheeled away, jaws clamped, eyes bleak with challenge.

That fool had taken him for his brother, Bufe — Bufe Telldane, the outlaw!

There'd been a time when Dane would have been quite pleased to be thought that brother; but that was past. Dane didn't hold with outlaws, nor with their violent, tumultuous ways. But convincing others of this had been something beyond his power. "Telldane?" they'd say when they heard his name. "Oh . . . yes. Telldane." And they'd give him a meager nod and thereafter leave him alone. Leastways, most of them did. A few tried to hire his guns; and sometimes he would bitterly curse Bufe Telldane for this blight he had put upon him. It was too like the fate of that guy in the poem — the one with the bird round his neck. It was like a spur to Dane, this rep of Bufe's; driving him into doing things sober judgment would not have condoned. But he viewed life now with a clearer perception than had been vouchsafed him at first. He understood there were some things a man couldn't stomach, and his condemnation of Bufe wasn't as strong as it had been.

But thinking got a man nowhere. He was daubed with the same black hate that had

11

pushed Bufe beyond the pale; and he must watch his step or, like Bufe, he'd be joined with the gunfighter breed.

The muscles along his lean jaw bunched as he thought of the cattle kings and their ways. Everything asked but no quarter given; and they'd always hired guns to bark for them — to take by might anything fair play denied them. Dane held no brief for the gunfighter breed, but he hated the cattle kings' guts. Hated them individually and collectively with a deep abiding rancor that could know no ease, no swerving. They were above the law; but they could turn that law to good account when they wanted some small-spread rancher moved, or when their own got into bad trouble!

He shook his young shoulders impatiently, the bitterness on him that always came whenever he thought of big Bufe. A fine upstanding man, Bufe had been, a bold and handsome fellow with a sparkling eye and ready grin . . . What was become of that grin now? What was become of Bufe?

Halfway down the block Dane was when a wheezy voice called out his name. "You, Telldane — come over here!"

He did not turn at once for experience had taught him one of the oldest tricks in the killer trade was to yell out a name and let whang. He stood perfectly still for a moment, and when he turned his eyes were wary in a face gone wooden, inscrutable.

Across the way was a man so vast every breath shook him like jelly. He had round freckled cheeks bulged out in a grin; and he waved when he saw Telldane looking. "Come over here. Let's git inside out of this —"

Dane lounged over and with risen vigilance followed the man inside the town's only adobe. It was a long and squat, quite solid affair, low-roofed; dimly cool after the glare of the street. A barroom it was, and well patronized even at this hour. Along its crude counter sprawled seven or eight men. The fat man went on past them, ignoring their desultory nods and trite words. He rounded the bar and threw open a door, nodding Dane through, the while he called back for a bottle. The bottle was brought by the bartender and plunked on the table with a pair of small glasses alongside. The fat man waited till the fellow had gone. Shutting the door with his boot he said, "Set down an' make yourself easy. My name's Rolsem, Major — in case you don't remember me. Hake Rolsem; an' glad I am to see you."

Dane sat gingerly down upon a chair's

edge with his right hand convenient to holster. "Yeah?"

Rolsem picked up the bottle; poured. "You're wonderin' what I got you over here for. I'm goin' to tell you directly," he promised, looking up with a grin. "But first: How long you been in this country — I mean to say, when did you get here?"

This fellow, Dane knew, was up to something. Something sly and foxy. It was there in the glint of his too-small eyes; in a number of things Dane was quick to peg. It made him reticent with his answer. He said, "I just rode in."

Which was true enough.

"Then you ain't — But no of course you ain't," Rolsem muttered; and sat a bit, twiddling his watch fob. He said abruptly, bluntly: "Jupe Dolton didn't send for you?"

"Dolton?" Dane searched his memory. "Never heard of him."

"He's a hound-low, stinkin' —" The fat man choked if off and rasped a pudgy hand across his chins as though worried. But Telldane's unconcern appeared to reassure him. He shrugged and blew out a sigh. "A man never knows who he's talkin' to. Jupe's a rustler and a goddam fool — been raisin' hob with the railroad, stoppin' its trains an' — You see that engine puffin' out there? It was carryin' the third Comp'ny pay roll that's been shipped this week. Jupe got it, like he got the others —"

"Stuck it up, eh?" Dane smiled faintly.

Rolsem's head bobbed up and down and his heavy jowls shook like a Saint Bernard's, and the black scowl riding his face seemed to Dane to be disproportionate to the amount of his interest. Dane said, "There's a lot of money back of that road —"

"You wouldn't think so," Rolsem snapped, "if you could hear them goddam hunkies! Frisby's section hands are threatenin' to quit an' —"

"Sounds like you might have a stake in that road —"

"Well, ain't I? by God, *ain't* I? Ain't I been follerin' them tracks all across this blisterin' country? Ever' time that slat-sided fool puts his gun on them trains it's just like liftin' the money right outa my pocket? Got a stake! I hope to tell you I got a stake! I say —"

"Let me have a say for a spell," Dane grunted. "What's this got to do with me?"

"I'm gettin' to that," Rolsem grumbled. "Sit down — sit down. Don't git impatient! I got to know first if Jupe's passed the word —"

"He ain't passed nothing to me — I

15

don't know him. Don't even want to know him."

The fat man seemed undecided; sat scowling at Dane suspiciously.

Dane got up.

"Hey — wait!" Rolsem blurted. "If you'll gimme your word —"

Before Dane could give him anything somebody knocked on the door.

With a badgered twist of his shoulders the man set his glass down and waddled over, groaning and grunting and muttering under his breath. But he stepped back quickly when he saw who it was, and an oily smile rubbed off his frown. "Come in! Come right on in. Rail — an' glad I am to see you. Here — wait; lemme close that door. Got a fella here you'll want to meet." He chuckled, rubbing his hands together. "Friend of mine — you prob'ly heard of him; Major Bufe Telldane. Major," he said, beaming, "Major, shake hands with Railhead Frisby."

Frisby was a broad and thickset man with a squat, scarred pipe in his teeth. His jaws were big, burly — like his arms; and the thrust of his teeth was belligerent. A fighter's face. Sun and the winds had wrinkled it, burned it dark as old leather. But a twinkle lit the hard bright eyes that were looking Telldane over.

16

Dane returned his stare with interest.

He had heard of Railhead Frisby. A man who got things done, they said. When anyone mentioned Rock Island, folks thought right away of Rail Frisby. Two thousand miles of steel were back of him; and they said the man wouldn't quit till he hit the Pacific Ocean.

Frisby chuckled like he'd read Dane's mind. "It ain't been no bed of roses," he admitted; "an' it's gettin' worse every day." Cold eyes brighter he stuck out his hand. A surprising thing, for most people when they heard the name Telldane froze up and stayed that way. About to mention he was neither Bufe nor this Rolsem's "friend," Dane said instead on impulse: "How are you, Frisby? Hear you been havin' some trouble."

The boss of the Rock Island nodded. "Can you use some work?"

Rolsem, who had been fiddlefooting round in his chair, said eagerly, importantly: "I jest been tellin' him 'bout the hell Jupe Dolton's been raisin'. He didn't know a thing about it — said he hadn't heard of Jupe —"

"That right?" Frisby's stare changed subtly. He said to Dane, "Shouldn't wonder if he puts us out of business — temporarily.

Bound to, if he keeps this train robbing up. We can't get any money through an' all my boys are kicking. Jupe's a tricky devil — I give him credit. Knows this country upside down; shakes every posse that goes after him. You say you're looking for work, Major?"

"That depends," Dane said, reacting to Frisby's words much as Bufe might have done. He pulled off his gloves, sat flexing long fingers leisurely. "Mebbe you better elucidate some. Haul round an' start at the beginnin'."

Approval showed through Frisby's glance. "Fair enough," he said, and told his tale with brevity. Jupe Dolton was a two-bit cow thief who had suddenly got ambitious. He had tried his hand with a train or two and then had gone after them serious. A handful of logs rolled across the track on a curve or an upgrade. That was his method; and very effective. Sometimes the man had helpers; these had been seen in the brush off-side overlooking the job with rifles. Jupe had met with little resistance. Three killings and a half-dozen hospital cases was the Dolton gang's tally to date.

"Used to be we could stand it," Frisby said, smiling wryly. "He'd let us get by with a pay roll or two. But late-like he's

18

taken to grabbing off every one. The whole damn road's setting up a howl, from the President on down; and if I don't get some money here pretty damn quick I'll be left to lay track by myself."

"Might take off a little of that weight," Dane said; but Frisby didn't smile.

"I'd like to see Jupe Dolton planted or hung up onto some Christmas tree," he growled. "He's lifted nine pay rolls off of us now, and no road under God's heaven can stand any draining like that."

"No," Dane said, "I guess not."

He picked up his gloves and saw the glint of the railroad boss' eyes change again. "Wouldn't you care to try your hand?" Frisby wondered.

"Afraid not. It's kind of out of my line."

"I wouldn't quite say that," Frisby told him. "An' you haven't heard all the story —"

"I'm still listenin'."

"Jupe is kind of a native product. Born and bred right here. His old man had a ranch of sorts — on the Canadian, up in the hill country. He got rubbed out, they say, in a brush with rustlers five or six months ago. His widow, Jupe's mother, took over the place along with a bunch of plasters. The old man had got in pretty deep."

19

"Jupe's mother runnin' it now?"

"Tryin' to, I imagine. They say Jupe's been keeping her in funds —"

"He ain't holin' up at the ranch, is he?"

"If he was," Frisby snorted, "he'd of had his neck stretched long ago. No, he stays hid out in the hills."

"What's the matter with your sheriff?"

"Nothing. Stroat's sound — square as they make 'em." Frisby knocked the dottle from his pipe and repacked it, his regard of Telldane quietly thoughtful. He seemed to be searching for something and, abruptly, to have found it. He leaned forward.

"If it's money —" he began, and stopped, alertly watchful.

He'd no way of guessing what sore spot he had prodded; no means of understanding what had shoved that sudden flare to the eyes bent cold upon him.

He saw only the baleful stare of a man with a chip on his shoulder. He supposed, of course, he was talking to Bufe Telldane, who was a hired-gun hombre by public knowledge. He did not look quite as old or as tough as Frisby had imagined, but the stamp of the breed was plainly on him and Frisby's experience with such gentry had proved them never to be allergic to the lure of ready cash.

So he said again, "If it's the money, why —"

"To hell with your money!" Telldane exploded as if he would hurl it in Frisby's face.

Rolsem whirled clear around in his chair, plainly expecting violence, and with his worried stare gone fixedly on Telldane — gone wide with incredulity.

But Frisby kept his place and kept his head, his eyes roving Telldane's gear, noting the condition of it. The blue shirt, twin-rowed with silver buttons; the Levis and tiger-snake hatband appearing to tell him much; and he nodded, even smiling a little.

"Sure," he said easily. "Damn it all you've a mind to. But when you've cooled off just remember the Rock Island road can pay with the best — can pay better. And *does.* I think you'd better work for us, Major." He let his grin stretch out a little. "After all, those indictments — Here! Hold on! Where you going?"

Telldane, fist on the doorknob, turned a face that was stiff with anger. "I'm goin' to rid myself of a stink!"

Hake Rolsem gasped.

Frisby's face went dark but he kept his temper. "You're turning my proposition down?"

"You're not talkin' to a scalp hunter, Frisby."

Frisby said, "This Jupe Dolton's a cheap killer. Shoots his —"

"I'm not interested."

Frisby's temper got the best of him then.

"If you won't work *for* us, then you're against us an' I'm going to act according —"

"Write your own ticket!" Telldane snapped; and barged out, slamming the door.

2

Last of the Doltons

Mad clean through was Dane Telldane when he slammed out of Rolsem's bar. Mad with a pent-up anger that had been bottled inside him for months. Mad with a maelstrom of seething passion that needed but a cockeyed look, but the drop of a hat, to explode him into violence. Mad, Hake Rolsem said, as a hatter!

Many factors contributed to the rage that roweled Dane; but the chief one was injustice — the injustices he saw all around him: scheming, little tricky men in places of public trust; crooked star packers; corrupt courts; oppression of small independents by the barons of money and influence. And this tale of Jupe Dolton —

"Pah!" Dane spat in the dust and stamped on. He yanked his gear off the corral fence, saddled his horse and mounted. "Gunfighter breed!" he snarled through bared teeth, and spat again. But the bad taste stayed. Frisby'd put it there when he'd rammed out that price like a worm on a hook — like that was all Dane had been waiting for. Like he'd just as lief kill a man as not, just so he got well paid for it.

When the rage fog lifted from his stare at last, he was miles away and his horse was flecked with lather. The sun had bent low in the west; red as blood it loomed behind Corazon Peak — though of course Dane had no knowledge of its name. To him it was just another peak; and he was drained of feeling, morose and gloomy — not even caring where he was. He stared about him, eyes dull and uncomprehending, dog-tired. He was like a man new-loosed from a nightmare; but gradually the natural look of the man came back to pull the tautness from his cheeks.

His glance played round without crossing a recognized landmark, without seeing so much as one small thing that was familiar to him.

Off to the right in the dusk of a twilight slope, obscurely crouched among the trees' down-folding gloom, stood a tumble-down shack — a line rider's shanty with a sagging corral back of it whose poles time had bleached and twisted. A stringer of smoke curdled up from the chimney, and in the whopper-jawed corral a bone-rack nag stood drowsing hipshot. Other than these there was no movement; no sign of life or occupancy.

Dismounting stiffly Dane tossed reins across a rickety rail that ran the warped veranda. The crazy steps and bent porch planking groaned out a dismal protest as he dragged his spurs across them.

A screen door. Paintless, rusted, patched and bulgy, it gave no hint of the room beyond; naught could Dane glimpse through its cloaking red rust save where, at the bottom, his shadow cast a darker blotch that let him catch the edge of a woman's skirt.

Dragging off his hat he said gravely, "Howdy, ma'am."

No answer.

He tried again. "Anyone home? Man of the house around, is he?"

No luck that time, either. Must be hard of hearing, Dane thought. He called more loudly, "Is your husband home?"

"Go away!"

Dane stared. Funny kind of answer.

He tried to see her, to make out her shape or features; but the rusted screen made a perfect shield.

Uncommon odd, that voice. Pitched in a queer key, seemed like. Stretched thin with terror it sounded — frantic. Yet in it was a cold hard edge of danger that drove Dane back a step, protesting.

"But, ma'am —"

"Go away! There's nothing for you here — nothing here but grief and trouble. Can't you be satisfied with what you've done already?"

"But what have I done?" Dane cried, bewildered. "I only wanted —"

"I know what you want!" The voice seemed keyed to a greater strain; and suddenly the door was flung open and a rifle's bore was thrust within short inches of his chest. *"Get out."*

Uneasy, baffled, Dane stood where he was and peered at her. The unusualness of the situation held him tongue-tied in the rifle's focus. Nothing he could think to say seemed likely to have any weight with her. Obviously she believed him someone else; but how to convince her of her error?

At any rate he knew who *she* was! The girl he had seen at the Siding; but so much more slender now she seemed, so fragile and, God! how beautiful! Like a picture she was. Straight up; shoulders squared by the grip of some awful terror. Fright made wide her too-bright eyes. . . . She was beside herself.

"Go!" she cried. "Oh — *go!*"

It was a wail, a cry from the soul — hysterical. In another moment her frantic clutch of that rifle must surely loose death at him. He stood there rooted, unable to move. He could not bring himself to turn — or even start to turn; he *dared* not, lest in this fright he startle her into squeezing the trigger without intent.

Breasts heaving she cried huskily: "Quick! I'll not warn you another time! Ride off right now, I tell you, or I'll not be accountable!"

"But listen, ma'am —"

"Go now, I say! And tell Jack Ketchum —"

The strain had proved too much for her. Face parchment-white she slumped, collapsing abruptly across the threshold. And so sudden was her swooning Dane's quick hands could not stay her fall.

But he stooped, caught her up from the floor and, marveling at her lightness, carried her into the shack's single room.

Just inside the door, in a bunk to the left, a man propped up on an elbow stared with flaming eyes across a pistol. But Dane, beyond that one questing look, paid no heed to him.

He carried the girl's limp shape to the lower of two bunks built against the rear wall — the upper held a sheeted figure. As Dane bent, gently lowering her, her eyes came open. Mutely she lay there staring up at him, brown eyes regarding him without luster; resigned, gone hopeless.

He stood by the bunk looking down at her. He didn't get this yet. But he'd seen quite enough to know these people were desperate. Apparently there'd been some kind of fight here. That man in the bunk was wounded — feverish, if one could judge by the look of his eye. And that sheeted shape . . .

He found the girl still regarding him; and more sharply now, more interested. He said on impulse: "I don't savvy the lay of this, ma'am, an' you've got no need to explain things. I'd like for you to know, though, I didn't have any part in it —"

"All right," came the growled, uncompromising tones of the man on the bunk behind him. "You've spoke yore piece — now git aboard yore bronc an' drift!"

Dane did not even look at him; but he put that tone away in his mind. He spoke to the girl: "You reckon to be all right now, Miz? — Sure you don't want I should ride for a sawbones?"

"No — oh, *no!*" she cried, starting up.

28

Dane dropped a hand to her shoulder gently. "Better you should set a spell there, ma'am, till you get rested. I'll take a look at —"

"You'll be takin' a look at *hell* if you don't git outen here pronto!" cried the man on the bunk in a fury.

Dane turned then, taking quick stock of the fellow. A lank and saddle-drawn man with the stamp of the long trails on him. He had a reckless face sharp-scowling from a tangle of yellow hair that was wantonly smeared across sullen brows that fiercened the blue of hunted eyes. A dangerous temper as great as Dane's own stared out of that face; and a bitterness that was greater.

"All right, Dolton," Dane said. "What's eatin' you anyhow, hombre? In a lather to cache that pay roll you lifted from the train this mornin'?"

The fellow shot straight up on the bunk, and the gun in his hand stopped wabbling. Its bore pointed straight at Dane's chest, and the flaming stare above it slitted. "So you know me, eh?" Jupe Dolton purred; and Dane braced himself, expecting a bullet.

It was what he hadn't expected that happened.

29

The girl came at him with the leap of a tigress. Before Dane could duck or could swing to fend it she had a strangle hold round his neck — a rough, deliberately choking one that got tighter every split second. And the wounded man, dashing off his covers, came slamming forward to make sure it took.

Dane Telldane lost his temper — completely and furiously. Without further care for the sex of this girl he drove broad shoulders hard to the left. The girl's clutch slipped. Before she could take up the slack Dane dropped low — dropped low and bent double. The girl went over his shoulders screaming; struck Dalton square in the chest. Struck him head on and took him down with her, cursing.

When they clawed from the sprawl Dane was holding a gun.

The look of his cheeks was plain warning. "Set down on that bunk an' stay there — both of you! I've had all the horse-play I want for one evenin'." He glared at the panting, disheveled girl. "I came here huntin' some grub an' a lodging —"

Dolton sneered. "An' guessed who I was first pop, eh?"

"It happened that way," Dane said coldly.

"Stow it! Take me in if you want yore damn blood money!"

Temper rocked the set of Dane's features; but he checked the hot words crowding his teeth, bit down on them eying Jupe furiously. "One fool in this place is enough!" he thought grimly, and said:

"I'll apologize to the lady. I'm sorry I had to handle her rough, but she asked for it jumpin' me that way. As for you — I've things a heap more important to do with my time than worry over any price *you'd* bring! I'll be sayin' good night to the both of you."

"Figure it'll be safer to lay outside an' pot me eh?"

"Why, you miserable whelp! My name is *Telldane* and the Tell—"

"*Telldane?*" Jupe's mouth fell open. Then the reckless glint of his eyes got brighter and he came off the bunk with a cat-quick grace and thrust a rope-scarred hand at Dane. "By God," he said, "put 'er there!"

He couldn't seem to credit it. "Telldane!" he repeated wonderingly as Dane let him pump his hand.

Dane knew what he was thinking. "My name," he said dryly, "is *Dane* Telldane."

But Jupe wasn't to be put aside that way.

There was only one Telldane in the country, and everybody knew it. If this guy wanted to call himself "Dane" that was quite all right with Jupe. He could call himself Archie Percival, just so he threw off his bedroll here.

He cried enthusiastically, "By grab, I never dreamed to meet up with *you!* Hell's hinges! Some luck — eh, Dulcey? Just the kind of fellow we're needin'."

Dane heard little of the fellow's talk; he was watching the girl. He had reckoned at first she was young Dolton's wife; but he guessed now she was his sister, and somehow the idea pleased him. Dulcey, with a hand to her breast, was darkly looking back at him; then her interest faded and she turned so that he saw her profile as she stared hopelessly at the sheet-covered figure in the bunk.

Jupe saw that look and swore. His glance became incalculably hard, and he said vindictively, "Never mind. I'll be payin' 'em off!" And he glared like a cornered lobo. Then he caught Dane watching him and a bitter sigh welled out of him. "It's Mom," he muttered drearily. "She's dead."

The girl without looking up said: "They killed her. Yesterday — yesterday evening. Ketchum's gang did."

"Just as sure as if they'd clapped a gun to her!" Jupe snarled.

The girl watched Dane. "It was her heart," she said. "It's been bad for years. The excitement —"

"But they'll pay!" Jupe gritted. "By God, they'll pay! I'll even this off with Jack Ketchum if it's the last thing I do in this life!"

Dane caught at the name; it was the one the girl had thrown at him. "Is that *Black* Jack Ketchum you're talkin' about? The Texan? Brother of Sam an' —"

"Brother of the devil!" Jupe snarled; and his lips peeled back. "You know him?"

"I know Sam an' Barry," Dane said. "Never met Jack, but many's the night I've spent at Barry's horse ranch down on the —"

"Yeah!" Jupe growled. "A pack of thieves — like all the rest of them Texans!"

"Suppose," Dane urged, "you tell me about this business."

"Why not?" Jupe said, and shrugged at the girl's cautioning look. "Mebbe," he said, "Telldane will help us —"

"Don't count too strong on that," Dane warned. "But I'd like to —"

"Well, the yarn's short an' soon told," Dolton muttered. "For three-four months we been losin' stock —"

"Jupe! Don't!" the girl said. "Don't tell him! Use your head and play this safe. You don't know —"

"Ah, to hell with safety!" Jupe sneered. "The only safety I'll ever know is what my six-gun'll get me! I've played safe too long already. If I'd had the backbone of a louse —" He broke off, eying Telldane darkly. "If you're backin' Ketchum this'll be no news to you; but if you're — Ah, to hell with it! Listen!"

He unfolded the luckless story.

Two years ago the Doltons — Jupe's dad had been alive then — had owned an up-and-coming cow spread in the hill country north of Logan: the Rafter. A day came when discovery showed their four-footed income to have dwindled by some hundred-odd head of prime beef. A vigilant check was kept in the next six months, that revealed a continuing and much more alarming loss. It was plain that rustlers had moved in on them. There was no calf crop at all, to speak of; and between the spring and fall roundups that year the Rafter had lost close to a hundred and fifty critters. That, Jupe's father had growled, was coming it pretty brash. He made public proclamation that either the rustling would quit, and pronto, or the mountain spruce would sprout hemp fruit. War talk, that; and the war had come. The thieving got immediately worse and three weeks later the Rafter crew caught a stranger red-handed touching up some Rafter brands. The man had laughed at them and died with his boots on — silent. The Rafter men took to combing the hills, determined to round up every strange rider who could not give thorough account of himself. But, though they hunted diligently and long, they caught no more long-loopers. Return to the home spread found ranch headquarters gutted. Every building had been burnt to the ground; there was not one post still upright in the corral. Fortunately Jupe's mother and Dulcey had been off in Logan visiting; but they found the cook's remains in the charred debris of the cook shack.

With headquarters removed to their present location — this line camp — things simmered along for a spell without any further excitement. Then came Alex Stroat one day — the Quay County sheriff — with a warrant for young Jupe Dolton. The charge was rustling and the evidence, Stroat said gravely, looked almighty convincing. Jupe's dad wasn't home and Jupe, on a rageful impulse, yanked his gun, tied the sheriff securely, and took out in haste for the timber: about the worst thing he could have done, he now admitted. Three days later his dad was found shot and with his head bashed in.

"Who stumbled onto him — an' where?"

"One of the Rafter punchers did. It was along out western drift fence. Just about," Jupe added meaningly, "a short six mile by crow flight from Jack an' Sam Ketchum's ranch."

"Had the Ketchums been round here long?"

"Not more than a couple weeks. Great bunch for ridin' — they ain't hardly been seen in town at all. Seemed like any time anyone seen 'em they was off somewheres on a horse. Ridin'est outfit you ever —"

"Well liked, are they?" Dane said, thoughtfully eying Dolton's gilt heels. "Get along pretty well with the local fry?"

Jupe shrugged. "I'll say this: they got the bes' damn horseflesh —"

Dane said "Yeah," and nodded, irrelevantly thinking of the man he'd met on the trail as he'd left the Siding. A rowdy-looking fellow with great burly shoulders that some way had reminded Dane of a man the Santa Fe authorities had last year grabbed — Deke Straper. Yet that could not well be, for Straper was in jail — the Santa

Fe pen's only lifer. A railroad telegrapher, Deke had been, and a good one; best man on the division till he'd gunned that fellow at Lamy.

Dane's mind roved on; then he said abruptly, "What kind of looking hombre is this Jack Ketchum? Tom's his right name, ain't it?"

"I dunno what his right name is; but he's a dark-faced, black-haired pelican with a set of lively features. Bold an' tough, if you get what I mean — an' big. He could bust you in two with his hands."

Telldane nodded. This Ketchum sort of sounded like one of the pair that, several days previous, had stopped a stage in the Steins Pass country. The law was hotfoot after them, and if Ketchum *had* been in it he'd be staying holed up for a spell. "What about Ketchum's outfit?" he asked.

"I don't know much about his men. No one does. They ain't been overcordial to callers. There's a guy named Franks in the outfit, and another squirt called McGinnis. The range boss' name is Trotter —"

"O.K.," Dane said. "What's the rest of it? You ain't mentioned the fight yet."

Jupe said affairs on the Rafter had gone from bad to worse. He wasn't accusing anyone, but after the old man's death the place went to pot in a hurry. Cattle took off wholesale. Three-four hands had asked for their time and Kling, the foreman, had let them go. Then Kling had turned up murdered and the rest of the crew quit right there. Mrs. Dolton and Dulcey — that was the girl's name, had stayed on; had hired a broken-down roustabout from up near Logan to help with what chores could be managed. Then *he* had been found a week or so later by one of Max Jackman's riders in the bottom of a gulch. Since then no man would work for Rafter and the women had been left by themselves. Jupe had helped out when he could, but mostly he'd had to stay hidden account of the Sheriff's scalp-hunting posses. "Since them Rock Island stick-ups," Jupe said, "they been after me hotter'n hell's backlog."

"Better leave the trains alone," Dane said.

"I ain't been near 'em — ain't never had the chance to be!" Jupe snarled. "But one of these days —"

"Sure. Where does Ketchum come into this picture?"

"I got an idee he tried to rig up some deal with the ol' man," Dolton said. "It wasn't long after that, that he was killed.

Paw, I mean. He'd taken to prowlin' round over at Ketchum's nights, an' I kinda figure they caught him up to it —"

"Six miles —"

"He wasn't killed where we found him. He'd been lugged there," Jupe said bleakly. He swiped the hair back out of his eyes. "I'm goin' to tell you somethin' — I don't expect you'll agree; but it's my notion Jack an' Sam Ketchum are the guys that been grabbin' them pay rolls. Now wait; don't butt in for a second. Up till last week I didn't have a smidgen of proof. Then one afternoon — I was hid out up in the Sierra Negras an', havin' nothin' better to do, was takin' a squint round through the glasses to see could I pick up any of Stroat's pelt-huntin' posses — I seen a dust springin' up just a little mite north of Obar. Five-six riders goin' like hell. An' back of 'em, mebbe eight-ten mile, was a second dust. I lost the first crowd soon's they hit broken country; but the secon' bunch kept rammin' north till they come right into my glasses. It was one of Stroat's posses, with Stroat rightup front lookin' mad enough to chaw a gunsight.

"First thing next mornin'," Jupe said, "I went over to where I'd lost the first bunch — same place Stroat had lost 'em. Fool

39

couldn't track a purple camel crost a snowbank! The sign was there, plain enough, an' I follered it quite a spell. When I lost it, 'long in the middle afternoon, I was within ten-twelve miles of here — *Get it?*"

He looked at Telldane meaningly. "The afternoon I'd watched these dusts was one of the days the Rock Island dropped a pay roll — to the 'Dolton gang,'" he growled bitterly. "Bet you anything you wanta name, it was the Ketchums held that train up. When I lost 'em them tracks was headed straight for Ketchum's ranch."

"That's hardly proof —"

"I know — I know!" Jupe muttered testily. "That's what I tol' myself. But I made up my mind I was goin' to have a gran'stand seat next time the Rock Island gave money away; an' by God I damn near done it!"

He had moved his camp in closer to Ketchum's ranch — the place belonged, he said, to Black Jack. During daylight he watched the spread with his glasses, keeping tabs on who came and went. And in the evening of the day before yesterday Ketchum's whole crowd went — in a body. Went south and east, with a mounted Jupe Dolton tagging.

But when darkness fell he had lost them.

He'd not dared stick close enough to hear the sounds of their travel. Night had hidden their trail away, but with the first light of yesterday's dawn he had taken up the trail again, following their sign impatiently. So enthusiastically, in fact, had he been following that sign that he had plumb overlooked the ample possibility that Ketchum's crew had not yet got under way. Such proved to be the case — they hadn't; they had camped the night in a rolling country some twenty miles south of the Siding. And Jupe, tracking them through the greasewood, had very near ridden smack into them. They'd been holed up in a little pocket, and one of their broncs nickered warning. "By God," Jupe said, "they come out of that pocket like sparks from the devil's anvil!"

There'd been no place for him to hide. The country was flat and the greasewood tops barely came up to a mounted man's shoulders. Jupe had dug spurs pronto. Bent low across the saddle he had used both quirt and steel and felt no shame in saying so. Lead had cut the brush all round him; but apparently Ketchum's broncs were still hobbled, for no pursuit had come after him.

Ten miles later he had climbed a low

knob and scoured the back trail with his glasses. But the only thing they had shown him was a faint dust drifting southeast. Gradually turning north it went until the sign pointed arrow-straight east.

"I did a pile of thinkin'," Jupe said, "an' the upshot of it was I rattled my hocks for Norton, figurin' they was strikin' for the railroad an' I'd mebbe cut their sign. But I didn't. They must of skirted the town. Just the same," he added doggedly, "it was Ketchum's crew, an' they was headin' for the R.I. tracks."

Dane considered, then shook his head. "Nope," he said, "that ain't enough. If you packed that yarn to Stroat he'd say you hadn't no case at all." He eyed Jupe speculatively. "By the way, is Stroat square? Is he on the level — honest?"

"Oh, he's honest enough," Jupe snorted. "He's too mule-headed to be anything else."

He got up off the bunk, took a turn or two about the room with his hands jammed hard in his pockets; scowled from a window at the darkening night. Wheeled back and, ignoring the girl's low protest, said: "There's a little more. I ain't told you about that fight yet. I fooled away considerable time tryin' to pick up their sign again, but finally I quit. I figured I'd come home for a meal an' see how things was here. I got in about five last evenin', an' I hadn't been here no time when who should come joggin' into the yard but Black Jack Ketchum himself. An' his crew of gunslicks was with him."

Dulcey nodded confirmation. "I went to the door," she said, "at his hail. He said he wanted to see Jupe a minute. I told him Jupe wasn't here. He just grinned and winked and some of his men started laughing. He said he guessed he'd see him anyway, and if Jupe wouldn't come out he was coming in. 'His bronc's here,' he said; an' he's here — I ought to know; we been trailin' him.' "

"An' without any more chin music," Jupe said, "he told his men to fan out an' cover all sides. 'What's the idea of that?' Dulcey asked him. An' he says: 'Jupe's gettin' to be a public menace, stickin' up these newfangled trains an' all, an' we're jest allowin', ma'am, it is time he was grabbed an' took in.'

"I could see right then it was neck meat or nothin'," Jupe growled. "He'd spotted me yesterday mornin' when I cut an' run for it, an' he was here to settle my hash. He told Dulcey if she didn't want to git hurt she'd better get the hell out of this cabin because he aimed to start borin' holes through it with his .45-90 rifles. Dulcey told him she wouldn't budge, an' Black Jack says: 'O.K., boys. Start cuttin' that shack to pieces.' "

"An' they didn't waste no time." Jupe went on. "First volley damn near lifted the roof off. I could see I'd have to run for it. I couldn't risk havin' Mom an' Dulcey shot up; an' I couldn't hold Ketchum off no-ways.

"My bronc was out back an' one of Jack's men had his eye on it. He riz up quick as I shoved a leg through the window; but I shot first, an' before the rest of 'em got on to what was happenin' I was on that horse an' battin' hell through the timber. They hunted me half the night pretty near, but I finally lost 'em in the Si-erras. I'd just got back an' found Mom dead when you come."

"What did you come back here for? I should think this was the one place you'd want to steer clear of —"

"Sure. That's why I came. I figured Stroat would take the same view you did. But never mind that. What do you think about them Ketchums now? Don't you reckon they're in on them robbin's?"

Dane turned it over. "It looks like it," he

44

said quietly. "But looks is a long way from provin'. On the face of it you've got a pretty fair case. But nobody'd ever take your word for it, an' you ain't got no proof; an' even if you did have you wouldn't get no chance to come out with it. They've got you pegged for a killer, boy, an' they'll open up on sight. What's more, if this yarn's true, you'll have Ketchum doggin' you, likewise."

"You aimin' to call me a liar?" Jupe blazed.

"No," Dane said; "I believe you. But that won't be helpin' you any. A Telldane's word won't bolster your story none —"

"Mebbe not," Jupe growled, "but his guns would sure strengthen my hand a heap. Look here, fella. How about throwin' in with me? I ain't got nothin' to offer, but —"

He broke off, gone stiff and gone listening.

Telldane, too, showed a sudden tautness.

There was hoof sound in the night outside — lots of it. Coming their way. *Fast.*

3

At the Rafter

Telldane whirled, and a stiff shove sent Jupe spinning toward the window. "Climb into your hull an' get goin' — I'll take care o' this!"

"But he can't!" Dulcey cried. "His wound —"

Telldane snorted. "Rode in here, didn't he? Then he can rack a saddle out of here — an' you better rack it quick," he snapped at the yellow-haired Jupe, "unless you crave to be tree fruit. Go on! Clear out! Get goin'!"

He watched Dolton's shape slam across the sill, then he turned to the frightened girl. "Your brother may be hurt, ma'am, but he'll be more comfortable in a saddle than he will if these comers catch him. No matter what you and me may think, the rest of this country reckons him the man that's been snatchin' the Rock Island pay rolls."

Through the gloom he saw her nod. In a voice deep-worried but brave she said, "I'll light the lamp. Whoever is coming might think it odd if they found the place in darkness —"

"Might think it odder if they found —"

"No," she said. "Mother and I always kept the place lighted. She always said it would be a comfort to Jupe if, hid off there some place in the mountains, he could look down and see our light."

The shadows swirled as she crossed to the table. The scratch of her match was a tiny sound low-rasped through the drumming hoofs. Its light burst red, turned yellow as it touched the lamp wick. Her light brown hair was a halo about her silhouetted head as she carried the lamp to a wall bracket. Her face was still pale when she turned, but she had gotten herself in hand again. There was a gallant courage in her composure.

Dane had been thinking. "Who furnished the evidence of rustling that supplied Sheriff Stroat with Jupe's warrant?"

"Jack Ketchum. Sh-sh! They're here!"

They were indeed. Dane could hear them dismounting in the yard. There was a mutter of voices, then heavy boots struck echoes from the porch. The door was pulled open and a man stepped in with other men crowding his heels.

He wore a gabardine jacket and a white shirt open at the throat. His legs were cased in whipcord trousers that were stuffed into fancy Hyer boots.

He removed his cream-colored hat to show hair that was dark and curling — hair deep-lustered with mahogany tints that would have been treasured by any woman. His teeth were white and even. They showed through the crack of his lips as his glance flashed briefly across Telldane. Then his gaze lifted, focused bodingly on the girl a second before, alarmed, it jumped to the covered shape on the bunk. "Good Lord!" he cried. "Don't tell me —"

"Yes," Dulcey answered. "Last evening." And she briefly recounted the story of Ketchum's raid.

During her talk disapproving mutters of sound burst impatiently from the newcomer's throat. When she'd done he said, patently exasperated: "He never should have come here — he knew better than that! I've warned him time and again! God only knows what might have happened — I tell you, Dulcey —" He shot a quick glance at Telldane and left unsaid whatever had been at his tongue's end. He said instead, "It's damnable — *damnable!* Why *won't* Jupe learn to use his head? If — Here," he told the men crowding the doorway back of him, "you fellows go on outside; I'll be with you in a minute."

His glance came back to Dulcey, flashed slantways to include Telldane. "Who's this?" he asked the girl. "What's he doing here?"

"Mr. Telldane," said Dulcey hastily, "shake hands with Mr. Jackman —"

"Telldane?" Jackman said, and his stare turned sharp.

Dulcey explained: "He's a friend of Jupe's."

"Jupe *would* pick a —"

"Just a second," Telldane drawled quietly. "The first name's *'Dane'* — remember it."

Jackman seemed about to snort, but curbed the impulse. The irritation that had scowled his glance fell away in a friendly smile that toned the squareness of his jaw and gave him a likable, tolerant look; and the feel of the fingers he closed round Telldane's hand was both vigorous and hearty.

"Glad to meet up with you, Dane Telldane. I'm range boss at the Square & Compass — my father's spread, you know. And it goes without saying any friend of the Doltons is bound to be a friend of mine — eh, Dulcey?"

The girl seemed a little embarrassed, but Jackman laughed it off. "Jupe's sister and I," he told Telldane, "are lookin' forward to traveling in double harness when all this trouble gets blown away and things settle back to normal. You figuring to be around, Telldane? Might be I could put you on —"

"Well, thanks," Dane said, "that's good of you. But I dunno. My plans are kind of hazy —"

"Well, if you happen to change your mind, let me know. Square & Compass could use another man or two — Shucks, Dulce!" He turned away from Dane. "This is tough on you. I wish . . ." His eyes went somberly across the room and he dropped a comforting hand to the girl's slim shoulder.

There was silence for a while and Telldane, observing, had to admire young Jackman's handling of the situation. You felt in his sympathy a lifting comfort, a well of strength that was yours for the asking. He wasted no breath in futile condolences.

Presently the girl's head lifted. She said bravely, "I'm all right now," and moved away to lean against the wall. "Luce, don't you think I'd better see Sheriff Stroat?"

"About Ketchum?" Jackman shook his head. "Not yet. No," he added definitely,

"I'd not go to him yet. Ketchum's hardly what you'd call a popular man; on the other hand, so far as is known, he's a person of integrity, a good ranchman, and a minder of his own affairs. If he employs a hard-case crew, these are times when that kind's necessary. If you come right down to a question of outfits, his crew's no worse than the average. They're better behaved than my boys. No — if you take this business to Stroat it'll be just your word against Ketchum's and, all things considered, he'll come off better than you will. Ain't that right, Telldane?"

Dane nodded. "Sheriff's bound to figure you've an ax to grind. I'd say sit tight. If Ketchum's our man a little more rope won't hurt him."

Jackman pulled on his gloves. He said to Dulcey, "Keep a stiff upper lip. We'll lick this yet. Tell your brother I said to lay low; and what I mean is *low*. He's getting too brash — a whole lot too brash. His best play is to hole up some place, and *stay* holed up till we give him the nod."

He caught Telldane's eyes and moved toward the door. Beside it he paused with a hand on the knob to say across shoulder to Dulcey: "You want I should send Hame Boswell out?"

The girl shook her head. "I — I guess we can manage." She crossed to the bunk that held Mrs. Dolton, sat down on its edge, shoulders drooped forlornly. Jackman beckoned.

Dane followed him out, closed the door and stood waiting.

Jackman led him off to one side, beyond the men's hearing.

"Look here, Telldane," he said grimly. "I'm bound to tell you this Ketchum business is not going to help Jupe any. It'll be one more nail in the top of his coffin."

"You mean . . ."

Jackman nodded. "Ketchum's been to see Stroat. I talked with Alex this evening; he's going to run Jupe harder than ever now. Ketchum claims Jupe broke into his place last night and tried to burn him out. Said Jupe fired a couple of his buildings. Says they saw him — recognized him plain in the light from the flames. Ketchum admits they exchanged a few shots. He says Jupe killed his cook."

Jackman was a black, stiff shape in the shadows. Telldane could not see his face, nor did he have to guess the man's expression. The grimness of Jupe's prospects was plainly etched in his voice.

Telldane said: "You reckon he's actually burned down a couple of his buildin's?"

"Why not? If he's the one that's really been stopping the Rock Island trains — Of course, I'm bound to say I'm not at all sure he is. It might just as well be Jupe — he's reckless enough to decide he might's well have the game as the name, and he's got the name already. But like I say, if it's really Ketchum that's back of —"

"Just a minute," Dane said. "Ain't it kind of risky of Ketchum to be callin' Stroat's attention —"

"You wouldn't think so if you were Ketchum. Jupe's been claimin' all along — even before he got himself outlawed — that Ketchum was back of old Dolton's killing. But the point I'm trying to make is that if Ketchum *is* the nigger in this wood-pile, he'll do what he has to, to get Jupe grabbed for it — to back his play. He's got to discredit Jupe's tale before Dulcey tells it; and the hell of it is that my say won't help her — I wasn't on hand when Jack came a-calling. And your word's no —"

"Yeah. We can skip that altogether," Dane said gruffly. He was recalling that Jupe had mentioned dropping a man when he went through the window. Ketchum's tale of Jupe's killing of his cook was to account for that man; and his naming of the fellow *cook* was very likely intended to

53

bolster his claim that the fight had taken place on Ketchum's ranch instead of, as it actually had, at the Doltons' Rafter line camp. The buildings, probably, had been burned for the selfsame purpose.

Jupe Dolton's prospects looked pretty black.

Dane said: "What do you suggest?" and his voice was cool as Jackman's.

The Square & Compass boss took a long time shaping his answer. When he finally spoke, it was to say, uneasy and worried: "I don't know, Telldane. . . . I don't know. Dulcey ought to have somebody round here; some man, I mean, to kind of keep an eye on things. I've tried to make her see it — tried to lend her one of my own men; but she just laughs. Declares no one would hurt a woman — actually seems to believe it! But this Ketch— Lord, I don't know *what* to say."

He paused with a glance sweeping Telldane's features. But the gloom that hid his own face must have shadowed Dane's as well. Jackman stood a moment silent. "If things was different," he said irritably, "I'd just as lief hire you to do it. But that's out, of course — unthinkable. A man of your rep hanging round —"

"Just suppose," Telldane drawled softly,

"you let Jupe an' me worry that out." Sarcasm put an edge to his voice. "I expect some polecats *would* think it queer for a woman to keep on way out here with nobody but a hard case round. Why don't you get her to put up in town?"

The night hid Jackman's flush but the feel of it roweled his tones. "There was nothing personal in what I said — God knows Jupe needs all the help he can get. I'd be the last —"

"I'm sure you would," Dane said dryly. "If that Boswell hombre you mentioned is a Boot Hill planter you better send him out here. That girl's in no kind of shape to undertake a burial. Have him bring the necessaries with him. Sooner we get this over, the better for all concerned."

Nodding, Jackman swung to his saddle. "Keep healthy," he said with a word to his men; and with a rumble of hoofs they were gone.

4

Cold Turkey

After they were gone Telldane remained awhile in the shadows, cheeks wrapped to a somber thinking. He was still there, still soberly reflective, when Dulcey Dolton called his name; called out to him softly, wonderingly.

Entering the house Dane closed the door and put his back against it. No words of his could change things, so he kept his place, shoulders stiffly settled, silent. As his glance played over her gravely it lightened and a kind of hope got into it. He meant her no discourtesy, no rudeness; it was only that he found her good to look upon and saw no need for hiding the fact.

She may have misunderstood. She turned, but instantly came round to find him with a scrutiny gone dark, gone searching. He knew this was appraisement; that she was weighing him, was judging him by what standards life had taught her. Yet the verdict stayed beyond him, was not to be read or guessed at, was not to be foretold.

She said hesitantly: "I — I expect you're considerable hungry. I'll scrape a bite together while you're putting up your horse. That is — you *will* stay, won't you?"

Dane nodded and went out.

They sat the solemn night through beside the sheet-draped bunk. And with the dawn Dane roused and groggily got up from his chair. He went, stiff-legged, to the creek and ducked his head in its icy waters and returned, if not refreshed, at least alert to a new day's forecast.

The girl had got a fire going in the stove, was busying herself above it. But Dane shook his head to her question, declining the food she would have fixed him.

"I'm goin' to town — to the Siding, if you'll tell me how to get there."

Despair loomed plain in the look she flashed him. A more knowing man might have taken comfort and flattery — might have taken, perhaps, satisfaction — from that knowledge. But precious little had been the time spent by Telldane in women's company; he hadn't the background to gauge the depth or guess the meaning of that look.

He saw only that she was afraid and shaped his words to reassure her. "I been figurin'," he said gruffly. "You need supplies

— more food, more cartridges. An' there's two-three things I got to tend to in that town before I quit it. I'll breakfast there an' be back by noon."

She would have kept him — the wish was strong in the stifled sound of her dismay. But she had perception, a judgment sharp, fine-ground by grim experience. Long acquaintance with a brother had given her insight — had taught her much about men's ways. They lived by rules not shaped to women's guidance, rules geared to some logic beyond the grasp of woman's understanding. There were things they must do . . . You dared not dissuade them.

Dark-eyed, troubled, she nodded mutely, masking her fears behind some portion of that deep, transcending courage that had served to lift and sustain her through the tragedy of death. Never again could she know a mother's counsel. Death had scrubbed the slate, wiping out the landmarked patterns that had shaped her to this hour. She was alone.

Alone . . . Not even Jupe could help her now. He, too, was gone; a phantom of the wastelands, a lorn and solitary rider — a puff of dust upon some trail.

Or dead — stark-sprawled among the windswept hills.

No! God would not have it that way. She closed her eyes and prayed. This man — this Dane Telldane — would somehow find a way to save him, would cut the toils their enemies had fashioned — would some way save Jupe from himself . . .

She opened her eyes and found Dane gone.

Dane found Sheriff Stroat in Rolsem's saloon. The triple-chinned Hake himself introduced them. With the sheriff's gone-hard regard intent upon him Telldane decided it high time a certain matter was straightened out. "My name," he told them plainly, "is *Dane* Telldane. It's neither Bufe nor Major —"

"Just what relation is there," Stroat wanted to know, "between you and the Major?"

"Bufe's my brother," Telldane said and eyed them bleakly. After a moment the sheriff nodded. "Fair enough. You figurin' to stay here?"

"Not right here," Dane answered, "but I'll probably be around."

"You got some special place in mind?"

"You got a warrant with my name on it?"

"No need to take that tone —"

"I take whatever tone best suits me."

The knuckles of the sheriff's hands showed white where they clutched his braces. Very gently then he slid those hands in calculated slant toward his gun belt; but when he got them there he shrugged. Telldane was darkly wheeling when Hake Rolsem blurted: "He turned down a job with Frisby yesterday!"

Instant quiet choked off all sounds but the metallic rasp of Telldane's spurs. He kept on toward the door.

"Hold on, Telldane!" the sheriff growled. "Is that right — what Hake just said?"

The curled look Dane put across his shoulder grabbed the lawman's gaze and held it. "I turned down the job Frisby offered —"

"What for? What kind of job?"

Dane was saying, "You'd better ask him —" when Rolsem cut in with a spiteful: "Rail wanted him to try could he catch Jupe Dolton!"

The sheriff's stare rasped bright and narrow. "An' what's so tough about —"

"Not a thing, Stroat. There ain't one angle to the business I'd describe as actually tough." Telldane, with his head tipped back, licked the smoke he'd rolled left-handed while his stare held the group by the bar.

"Then why —"

"Perhaps," Dane drawled, "I didn't care for its smell."

A deep roan grabbed the sheriff's cheeks.

"Mebbe I figured there was plenty houn' dogs a-nosin' that trail already," Dane grinned.

Stroat's face darkened with a yen toward violence. He took a half-step forward and his big hands clenched. "Put that plain —"

"I will. Did you furnish stars for that raid on the Doltons?"

The place had been quiet, but not like now. A tense hush gripped it and men hung poised like a chill had frozen them. Light gleamed in their eyes like sun on ice; and Telldane's drawl held the crackle of frost. "Did you send Jack Ketchum out there?"

"I didn't send anyone —"

"Well, Ketchum was there; and his hard-case crew. They undertook to smoke Jupe out. Mebbe their smoke got a little thick. When it cleared, Mrs. Dolton was dead." Telldane's gaze held Stroat's like a curse. "Must've taken rare courage to pull a stunt like that!"

The only sound was the rasping wheeze of the fat man's breathing.

Stroat's voice crossed that sound with a stark sincerity. "Good God, Telldane, I didn't know . . . I never dreamt —"

"Did you deputize Ketchum?"

"No; of cour— Wait! Yes. I did. Two-three months —"

"I mean yesterday."

"Certainly not! D'you think I fight women?" the sheriff spluttered, cheeks purple.

"I've hated to think so. But somebody's fightin' 'em — the same white-livered skunk that murdered Jupe's father and —"

"Hold on, boy — stick to the facts! You don't know anything about Ed Dolton's killin' — or *do* you?" Stroat demanded, eying Dane sharply. "In fact," he snapped, wits working again, "how do you know —"

"I was out there," Dane said, and the saloon crowd gasped. "Just what do you know about this fellow, Jack Ketchum? What —"

"Never mind that," Stroat growled impatiently. "I'll take care o' that. What I want to know is —"

"Then you better go see Dulcey Dolton; she can tell it better than I can. There's just one thing I want to make clear. The next gun throwers caught on that spread will be sifted."

Like that, Dane said it, and stepped through the door.

★ ★ ★

The first post office at Six-Shooter Siding (or Tucumcari, as the place is now called) was picturesque, to say the least. Half hidden among the clutter of dismounted boxcars, tents and tarpaper shanties that leaned every which way, it was made of hastily ripped apart packing cases that had, apparently, been even less carefully renailed together. But it was colorful — the most colorful place at the "end of steel." Tomato and apple and citrus labels checkered its walls with the crazy pattern of a Jacob's coat; and atop these, on the inside walls, in helter-skelter profusion, regulations and government notices had been tacked among reward bills, a few of these garnished with unrecognizable faces. And what few other places might have revealed bare wood had been enthusiastically hidden behind a heterogeneous collection of patent medicine advertisements guaranteed to cure all the ills of a gun-ridden country.

Telldane stepped in from the hot sun's smash and, ignoring the idlers, walked to the window in the partition that kept folks from helping themselves to the mail. A spectacled gent with a white goatee looked up from his sorting to see what Dane wanted.

"Postmaster here?"

"You're looking at him, suh. I'm the postmaster of this yere Siding. John Quincy Adams, suh — of Kaintucky. What can I do for you?"

Dane regarded him dubiously. "Well —"

"If you wanted to see me about that dang hoss of Eli's —"

"No horse," Dane said. "I was wonderin' if 'twould be all right for me to post a — well, a kind of public-private notice —"

"What kind's that?" demanded Adams, peering over his glasses. "If it's private, what you want to post it for? An' if it's public, how 'n Tophet do you figure it's private? I cal'late you must be lookin' for the —"

"Perhaps," Telldane smiled. "I had better explain. My name's Telldane — I'm foreman of the Rafter — the Dalton ranch up near Logan —"

The gasps of the loungers stopped him there. But he didn't turn. Grin gone a trifle tighter, he said: "What I want to do is post a notice concerning the ranch — that is," he added, "if you've no objections."

The postmaster stared a moment. "Don't know as I have," he said finally, and cocked his head at the plastered walls. "Post all you please, if you can find a place for 'em."

"One will be plenty. Got a sheet of paper?"

Adams found one. Tearing off the government heading, he pushed the remainder across the sill. "Got a pencil?"

"I could use one."

Adams supplied it and Dane, paying no attention to the whispered comments passed behind him, proceeded to draw up his notice. Handing back the pencil, he picked up the tacks the postmaster had gotten him and, using the butt of his six-shooter for hammer, tacked his comment right beside the window.

"Hey!" Adams cried. "Not there — Hell's fire! You've covered up the reward Stroat's offered for young Dolton —"

"Mebbe it needs covering up," Dane said, and went out.

Behind him the post-office loungers crammed excitedly about the window. But their perusal of the posted notice was somewhat retarded by the head of Postmaster John Quincy Adams which, thrust about the angle of the window, was not only first in place but first in sight of his countrymen. They fidgeted and squirmed but Mr. Adams read bug-eyed till, with a sudden inarticulate gasp, he snatched the obtruding head away at a speed little short of frantic. And hard on the heels of this astounding spectacle (for Mr. Adams never had been known to hurry) Mr. Isadore Jogglebaum, in town on behalf of Otero, Sellar & Company, Trinidad merchants, let loose a shout "Gott in himmel!" and departed the place as if a centipede had got up his pants leg.

Those who had to spell things out got their look at Dane's poster then. It said:

DUE WARNING

is served on all and sundry that hereinafter and starting now, any swivel-eyed polecat caught prowling Rafter range, or otherwise exploring Dolton property without good excuse or business satisfactory to the owners, shall be speedily and permanently disposed of by

DANE TELLDANE
Foreman of the Rafter

5

"Don' Argue!"

Telldane had talked cold turkey to the sheriff, but he was experienced enough to realize Stroat would be bound to weigh all he had said in the light of what Jack Ketchum had previously told him. Which was only fair; inasmuch as Ketchum, to the best of Stroat's knowledge, was an honest, upright rancher, whereas all adverse testimony against him would have come either from interested parties or from Telldane himself — whose word, the sheriff was bound to feel, he had ample reason for doubting. Boiled down, therefore, all that Dane's gassing with Stroat would amount to would be to publicly put him on record as partisan of a wanted outlaw. Stroat would stick to his original intention — would camp harder than ever on Dolton's trail. It was up to Jupe, in consequence, to keep himself out of Stroat's way.

Ketchum — if it really was Ketchum behind the Rock Island's troubles — looked to be a pretty slick article; and all Dane had ever heard tell of the Ketchums tended to confirm this impression. They were all horse ranchers, and rumor had long been rife in Texas that if you were on the dodge, or figuring to ride the River, the Ketchums were raising the kind of broncs you needed to keep the Law away.

Which was all to the good so far as it went. Trouble was, it didn't go far enough. Talk wasn't proof, and you didn't jail men just because you might happen to suspect them. Ketchum was playing a mighty shrewd game if he was grabbing the Rock Island pay rolls.

But Dane, in his thinking, found one queer thing. If Ketchum was the big dog back of things it looked like he would find Jupe worth a good deal more to him loose than dead or behind the bars. He would rep for Ketchum as cat's-paw, as scape-goat, only so long as his movements were subject for guesswork. Once let Stroat get Jupe behind bars and it would be at once plain — if the train robberies kept on — that Jupe was not the man backing them.

With the sack of supplies slung across his shoulder Dane was heading for the corral where he'd left his horse when two men stepped out of an alley and deliberately blocked his path.

Dane stopped.

If this were trouble they had him at a disadvantage. The sack on his shoulder was heavy and, intent on his thinking, he'd been using his right hand to hold it. And hereabouts, and at the moment, the street was practically deserted.

"Well?" he said. The two men grinned.

"Not bad," drawled the man on the outside, meaningly. He was long and dark with a lantern-jawed face, and calculating alertness was fused with the curiosity in the half-closed yellow eyes that were looking Dane over thoughtfully. "So you're Telldane — the guy that put up that sign." He made the words a statement and Telldane waited, silent.

The second man said: "Let's bust 'im, Morg, an' get done with it!"

This was the fellow Dane had met on the trail yesterday morning just outside of town. And Dane, eying him, was more certain than ever that here was Deke Straper who was supposed to be safely locked in the Santa Fe penitentiary. The man — if he wasn't Deke — was sure a ringer for him. Dane watched the pair of them hawk-eyed.

The tall fellow said: "Keep your shirt on, Chuck. Just let me take care of the talkin'." To Dane he said: "That was a kind of brash statement you put on that sign."

Dane said, "I'll back up any words of mine right now — or any other time."

Amusement gleamed in the tall man's stare, and he nodded. "My name's Trotter — I'm Jack Ketchum's foreman. Just a word of advice, bucko. You'll probably *have* to back 'em up if you're figurin' to camp at the Doltons'." And without more words he hooked an arm through the burly Chuck's and strode off toward the saloon.

Dane looked after them thoughtfully; slowly rasped his jaw. "So that was Morgan Trotter," he murmured. "Well, he puts things plain enough so's even a blind man could unravel 'em, give him time. Wants me out of the country, does he? Or is it Jack Ketchum that's nervous?"

It was something to think about; and he thought about the man who'd been with Trotter, too — the gent who looked like Deke Straper. For two cents he'd have wired Santa Fe to see if they had Straper in there.

But, Straper or not, it was plain to Telldane that Ketchum's crew — if these were a sample — need never apply to the employers of Bible tract salesmen.

Like Mr. Frisby's clothes, division head-quarters were quite apt to be wherever you

70

happened to find him. Sheriff Stroat found him giving hell to the track layers and, catching his eye, went at once to the point. "Did you offer a job to a guy named Telldane?"

Frisby looked at him sharply, then beckoned him off to one side. "I did," he said. "What about it?"

"Just what was the job you offered him?"

After a moment's consideration Frisby explained.

"An' he turned you down, eh?"

Frisby nodded.

"What was the idea puttin' that job up to him? That's sheriff's business an' —"

"Sure," Frisby said; "but it's a business too damned flourishin' to suit this railroad's directors. I can't lay track without a crew, and the crew I've got is threatenin' to leave me flat if I don't catch up on their pay. I don't doubt the beneficence of your intentions, Alex — I got good intentions myself; but this crew of mine ain't got no use for good intentions. They want hard cash an' want it quick! My business is to build this road, an' if you can't keep my pay rolls from fallin' into Dolton's hands I've got to —"

"By God," Stroat broke in with a savage oath, "I'll stop 'em! I'll damn well put young Dolton where —"

"Sure," Frisby said. "But when?"

The sheriff scowled. "I'm only human. I can't be —"

"Exactly! That's why I tried to hire Telldane —"

"Look here," Stroat said abruptly. "Does he strike you as the kind of man —"

"He does seem a little young," admitted Frisby thoughtfully. "I'd expected Bufe to be an older hand — but he's got the look, all right."

"What I'm gettin' at," Stroat interrupted, "is — do you think the fellow is Bufe himself or —"

"What's that?" said Frisby, eying the sheriff sharply. "I was introduced to him as Bufe —"

"I know. But Rolsem kind of stretched things some when he said Telldane was his friend. As a matter of fact, he tells me he never met the man but once, and that was several years ago. Telldane has give me to understand his name's not Bufe but *Dane* — says he's Telldane's brother."

Frisby stared. "I didn't know. Bufe had a brother."

"No more did I," Stroat grumbled. "But the question is, *if* Bufe's got a brother an' this guy *is* that brother —"

"Yeah. Kind of complicates things, don't

it? Still, I don't see that it needs to. This fellow — whoever he is — is plain enough a gunman. The trade sticks out all over him. Got that proddy look in his eye an' —"

Stroat waved all that impatiently aside. "The point is if the guy is *Bufe* I got plenty excuse to put him back of bars; but if —"

"If what?"

"If he isn't Bufe I'm not so sure," Stroat muttered. "I ought to run him in on general principles. Trouble is, he hasn't actually done anything yet I can take him up for — unless he's Bufe." He paused, looked at Frisby keenly. "I guess you ain't heard the latest. He told me not two hours back that he's going to sieve any guy caught prowlin' Rafter land —"

"That's plain enough," declared Frisby grimly. "If he's sidin' a wanted outlaw —"

"It ain't that easy, damn it! He's posted a notice to the same effect in the post office. But he's signed it, 'Dane Telldane — Foreman of the Rafter.' Which, goddammit, puts a diff'rent complexion on the business!"

In a few terse sentences he related what Telldane had told him regarding Ketchum's alleged raid on Rafter, "I doubt if there's a ounce of truth in it; but there *might* be. An' if ol' Miz Dolton's dead . . ."

He let the rest trail off and looked at Frisby worriedly. He said abruptly, savagely: "You see the way my hands are tied — damned if I do an' damned if I don't. I can't go yankin' Dulcey Dolton's range boss round just for tryin' to protect her interests."

Frisby's lips framed a dry, hard smile. "No," he murmured mildly. "Knowin' Telldane's backin' Jupe, an' *provin'* it, ain't like to be the same thing, hardly. Guess we'll have to give in he's outslicked us on this one. What do you reckon to do?"

"What," Stroat demanded, "*can* I do? Wait an' —"

"We can do a little better than that," Frisby mentioned. "Let me mull this over awhile, Alex. Probably something will come to me. There's some possibilities in that girl, I think. You go out an' look things over; see if the old lady's really dead." He eyed the sheriff thoughtfully. "You ain't puttin' no stock in that tale of Ketchum bein' back of these stick-ups, are you?"

"It don't seem no way likely."

"Well," Frisby grimaced, "you go take a squint around an' look me up in the morning. I'll have a talk with old Max Jackman —"

A rattle of pistol shots stopped him.

Both men wheeled, stares gone intent; even the section gang leaned back on its picks and sledges. The shots seemed to come from the far end of town. All along the street men were turning, staring worriedly toward the distant corral.

With a curse the sheriff departed.

Still thinking about Trotter's thinly veiled warning, and about the man who had been in his company and who looked such a ringer for Straper, Dane gave a hitch to the sack on his shoulder and struck off toward the corral.

Multitudinous things were afoot in this country and, to a man who could read the signs, a considerably stronger medicine was brewing. There was going to be trouble here — bad trouble. All the events of the past few months — loss of the Telldane ranch, Bufe's didos and all the rest of it — had sharpened Dane's faculties and perception to the point where he could see in a smile or the glint of an eye the unsaid things behind it. Conditions in the Tucumcari country were such as to prompt an instant suspicion of any stranger in the hair-trigger minds of its denizens. The stranger's hand was forced. Owl-hoot riders rode the trails, and to be unknown was to invite disaster; you must take one line or the other. You backed the law or you favored its breakers.

Dane was under no illusions on that score. Putting his name on that notice as foreman of the Rafter had lined him solidly with the Doltons; had dumped their feud with the law in his lap. It had been tantamount to espousal of their cause; he could expect the same kind of treatment from Stroat and the law as was being dished out to young Jupe.

Well and good — so be it. This would not be the first time a Telldane had burned his bridges to stand by an unpopular conviction. The law held Dolton guilty; Telldane took a different view and was prepared to back that view to the limit. He did not hold with the gunfighter breed but there were times when its methods commanded his grudging approval. Times like these when a man had no other recourse.

In the shape of this thing building up here Dane Telldane saw a familiar pattern — one made so by grim experience. And he had but one answer for it; the weight that joggled his thigh.

He stopped, poised stiff and breathless, as the pulse of heavy pistols quick-drummed through the rumbling of passing wagons and the continued sounds of carpentry. Like a window had been closed on them these lesser sounds dropped away as men suspended their tasks to listen — stopped their teams and stopped their sawing, dropped their hammers, or whatever else they had in hand, to turn and peer, still scowling, toward the poles of the yonder corral.

Dane let go of his sack and, with his thoughts on Dolton, broke into a lurching run.

Men stared; he heard some gasp as he pounded past them; but all his thinking was centered on the grim tableau that was got afoot off yonder in the slatted dust haze. Through its curling screen Dane glimpsed it — a half-dozen gun throwers savagely bent on murdering a man backed into the crotch of the pole enclosure. He didn't stop to ask if that lone man was Dolton; it made his blood boil just to see what odds they had stacked against him.

And those odds were intended to be kept as they were; Dane was given curt warning when two of the gunslicks whirled and sprayed a few slugs screaming round him. He ducked, threw himself to the right. A swift lunge put him back of a wall and he jerked his six-gun angrily.

But there was nothing for him to shoot at there; and the light from his slitted stare gleamed cold as windswept ice as he dived swiftly round the wall's far corner and was brought spang into the thick of it. He could see the lot of them now, vague-outlined in the swirling dust, ganged up to rush a quick victory. They were charging the man when Dane loosed a rebel yell high-yipping and drove thumbed shots that dropped the murder-minded crew in haste behind the corral's far side.

Flame burst luridly between the bars as they triggered to blast him down before the man they were after wriggled clear.

But the man showed no wish for bolting. From where he crouched Dane could see him plainly. It wasn't Jupe Dolton. A tall, big-boned sort of gent he was in brush-clawed 'Chihuahua finery. Color showed at his waist in a scarlet sash; and even as Dane looked the man leaped from cover and, with bared teeth, charged for an angle that would put his would-be assassins between Telldane and himself.

A bold move; but the bushwackers had no mind to be placed in such a crossfire. They scrambled up with shrill cries and through their ripped-out oaths Dane caught the blat of shouted orders — by his voice, knew the shouter instantly: Morgan Trotter, Ketchum's range boss!

Dane sprang forward, rushed the corral with the thump of lead spurting dust round his boots. He heard it smacking the wall behind. But he didn't stop — ran crazily on, straight into the crash of that triggered lead; and powder smoke strung from his own bent frame as the Colt-guns rocked his sweating palms.

His curled-back lips showed the glitter of teeth as he flung himself hard-on at the poles; saw the crouched men back of them spring to their feet and mill, frantic, bedeviled, their stark eyes bright as the beady stares of cornered rats.

Gunfighter breed! They could dish it out but they couldn't take it. They hadn't the stomach for a dose of their own. Caught in a crossfire they clawed for their saddles. Dane saw one man, with both arms flailing, jerk backward and skid from the rump of his horse. Another man, mounting, let go the horn with his mouth stretched wide in an unheard screech. Then the group was gone, was screened by the dust; all but the two still shapes near him.

Dane was starting toward them when a hard grip closed on his shoulder. A rough hand yanked him round and Stroat's face, stiff and livid with anger, showed blazing eyes but a foot from his own. Stroat's gun jabbed his belly. "By God," Stroat snarled, "there's a law in this town!"

Dane looked skeptical.

Stroat's anger choked him. "Head back uptown! You're goin' to jail!"

"Oh, no — not jus' now," a voice drawled coolly. "Get the han's up, meester. You're know me — *don' argue!*"

6

Overture to Violence

Dane twisted his head as the sheriff let go.

The man who had spoken was the dry gulchers' victim, the gent the dry gulchers had been trying to cut down. It appeared their attempt had been short of successful. His dark half-moon face showed big teeth in a grin. "You're know me," he repeated, and chuckled at Alex Stroat's cursing.

"Not expect for to see me this queeck, eh, compadre? Kin Savvy, she's no scare for shucks. You bet! Geef this hombre your gun an' start hikin'."

The sheriff hesitated, glared from the fellow's leveled pistol to the fellow's hateful grin. "You're not doin' yourself any favor, Kin Savvy, takin' up for this lobo. His name's Telldane an' he's sidin' Dolton —"

"*Pues,* me, I'm mebbe side Jupe Dolton too," the big Mex grinned. "He's — how you say? — one exciteful hombre. Any'ow," he looked at the sheriff again and shrugged, "this fellow jus' make the play for save Kin Savvy's breakfast. Them Black

81

Jack Ketchum, she try for rob me out."

"Rub you out! *Ketchum?* You must be smokin' rattleweed," Stroat growled, eying him sharp.

"I be smokin' *you,* come you don't shuck loose of that gon," Kin Savvy declared pointedly. Still scowling, the sheriff let go of his hardware. "You're goin' to rue this," he said grimly. "Half the town has seen this play —"

"Play? This no play — w'en Kin Savvy play, she play for keeps," the Mexican chuckled, and motioned the sheriff to be on his way.

Stroat's hard mouth locked bleakly — bleak as the look he gave them both.

Kin Savvy winked behind his back. But as soon as the sheriff took off, his round face sobered. "Queeck," he said, scooping up Stroat's gun. "I'm think thees good time for hurry."

They got their broncs and, without stopping to slap on saddles, they swung aboard and jabbed their spurs. As Kin Savvy had correctly implied, this was no time for picking daisies. Already slugs were screaming round them as townsmen ripped the quiet with hastily grabbed-up rifles. The sheriff would have plenty of help, now that the two were running.

But the time was past for grandstand plays; it was time right now to be moving.

They were six miles out with the posse well lost in the oak brush when Dane remembered his dropped sack of supplies. He pulled up with an oath that brought a quick questioning look from the Mexican.

With a scowl Dane told the fellow how he'd come in after supplies and then, in the excitement, had come away without them. "I'm roddin' the Dolton spread," he added. "Jupe's sister's all alone there an' she's a heap in need of that stuff. I don't know what you think about Jupe, nor anything about your politics except you're plenty handy with your iron. But I got to go back after that truck an' I don't cotton to leavin' that girl out there by herself a second longer than I have to."

He eyed Kin Savvy sharply. "Could I trust you to sort of go out there an' kind of hold things down till —"

The big Mexican showed his teeth in a grin. "*Seguro si,* amigo. Kin Savvy, she's onderstand. She's guess you think them Black Jack Ketchum mebbe go out there raise hell, eh?"

"What give you that idea?" Dane spoke a bit sharper than he'd meant to.

But Kin Savvy only shrugged broad

shoulders *"Quién sabe?"* he chuckled, wrinkling up his eyes. Then he tugged an end of his mustachio and with his other hand patted his pistol. "Them Black Jack no bother señorita. Go with God, my friend."

It was getting on toward sundown when Dane Telldane rode back into town. He rode in quietly, leisurely, as though without a care in the world. But he rode with hatbrim cuffed low-down aslant his eyes. He stopped by the corral and got his gear; swapped talk with the liveryman. But all the time his eyes were busy and he was not deceived by the man's elaborate casualness. The fellow recognized him sure as sin and would be hunting up the sheriff just as soon as he rode off. He debated the advisability of tying the fellow up; decided against it. He said instead: "Is the sheriff still around town?"

The man hadn't been expecting this and surprise dropped his jaw open ludicrously.

"Expect I'll find him in his office?"

"He usually eats about this time —"

"Where? I mean, which place?"

"Why there ain't but one — Lone Star Cafe."

"O.K. Much obliged," Dane said, and swung up into the saddle. He flipped the man a dollar and turned his roan up the street. When he came opposite the hash house he swung down and tied his roan beside others. Then he stepped up on the walk, reasonably certain that the man, now thoroughly fuddled, wouldn't be hunting up Alex Stroat.

He went into Goldenberg's general store and ordered more supplies. He came out with them sacked across his shoulder and then stopped short, face to face with the sheriff.

Stroat was surprised as he was. But only for a second. With a thin hard grin he said: "Just a moment, bucko. I want a word with you!" And, quick as light, his gun came out and focused on Telldane's middle.

A cool grin cut Dane's sandy jowls. "Fair enough. I want a word with you, too. Where can we talk?"

"Right down to my office," Stroat said, and motioned with his gun.

"Wait'll I get my horse —"

"You touch that bronc an' I'll sure let daylight through you!"

Dane looked at him. The sheriff was in earnest. Without further talk Telldane preceded the lawman down the street and stepped into the cubbyhole the sheriff used for an office. Setting his sack on the floor he folded his arms and stood against the wall.

"All right," he said, "let's have it."

"I aim to," Stroat said grimly, kicking the door shut with his boot. "Put your gun down on my desk —"

"I can talk just as good with it in my belt —"

"Any talkin' you do'll be to Circuit Judge Crans—"

"Oh, no, it won't!" Dane said, and with one clean uplifting sweep of his boot knocked the gun from the sheriff's fist. "Not so's you could notice it!"

The sheriff, face livid, closed in with clenched fists; but Dane was in a hurry. Any sound of a fight might bring aid to the officer, and he wasn't taking any chances. He whipped the gun from his own belt and brought its barrel down across Stroat's head. The sheriff went down like a poleaxed steer — and stayed down.

Dane lugged him into a cell and took the precaution of locking the door. Removing the key he laid it in a conspicuous place on the sheriff's desk and, picking up his sack, stepped out.

It was full dark when he reached the ranch.

A challenge stopped him in the yard. *"Quién es?"* a voice demanded.

"Dane Telldane," he said, and Kin Savvy stepped out of the tree gloom.

"*Bueno* — you get heem?"

Dane tossed him the sack and dismounted. "Miz Dolton all right?"

"*Seguro* — sure," Kin Savvy said, and with a grin added, "A leetle worried."

"That you, Dane?" the girl's voice called to him.

He could see her on the porch now, a dim, vague shape in the shadows. He picked up the sack and joined her. Her hands were cold to his touch. She did not speak till they were inside the house and she stood with her back to the door.

"Dane — Dane!" she said, and he could feel her shaking. "That man — that man out there — that Mexican! He's one of Ketchum's men!"

He found the lamp and lit it. Then he turned, eyes searching her face. He saw fear plain upon it — in the too-bright eyes, in the way her cheeks were blanched; and he cursed himself for a fool. "You're sure?"

She nodded emphatically. "He was with him day before yesterday when Ketchum came after Jupe. I know he was! I *saw* him!"

Dane strode to the door, yanked it open. "Kin Savvy!"

The big Mex dragged his spurs across the porch; stepped in. He put his back to the wall and grinned at Telldane knowingly. "The girl 'ave tell you?"

Dane said harshly: "If you've anything to say, say it quick."

Kin Savvy shrugged. "If she 'ave say I work for them Ketchum, *válgame Dios,* it ees true. But no more! *Sangre de Cristo, no!*"

"No?" Telldane's tone implied grim doubt. His eyes were bleak as agate. But the Mexican imperturbably returned the stare with the easy languor of his kind.

"No," he said. "Them Black Jack, she's try for take my scalp —"

"Yeah. A slick stunt!" Telldane's voice was sarcastic. "He wanted to plant somebody with this outfit, so —"

"She's sure want to plant *me,* all right," Kin Savvy chuckled. Growing serious then he tugged at his mustachio, considering the challenge in Dane's eye as though turning something over in his mind. At last, with an elaborate care, he laid his big six-shooter on the table and from his shirt pulled out a paper which he extended toward Telldane.

But Dane was not to be caught like that. It might be good or it might be bait. If it was bait Dane wasn't biting. "Take a look at it," he told the girl, and kept his glance on Kin Savvy.

He heard her opening the paper. "It's in Spanish," she said. "I can't read it."

Dane motioned toward the Mexican's pistol. "Let's see it. Hold that gun on him an' if he so much as blinks —"

"Caramba!" the Mexican cried. "You think Kin Savvy the fool?" But there was a glint in his eye despite the words; an amusement, and Telldane saw it.

"Be careful," he drawled, "or you'll be a *corpse*."

Then he dropped his glance to the paper. That first brief stare brought a whistle of astonishment from him. He looked up at Kin Savvy sharply. It was an official document that he held in his hands, and bore the signature of the commandant of Rurales at Agua Prieta.

All well and good so far as it went, but Kin Savvy's grin made him pause. He eyed the man through slitted lids and the corners of his mouth drew down with a quick suspicion. "So you're an officer, eh?" His laugh was short, without humor. "This thing might fool a man like Stroat, but it ain't pullin' any wool over *my* eyes. Shove up them paws an' keep 'em up!"

Kin Savvy with a resigned look of tolerance raised his hands. "You read the Spanish?"

"You bet! An' that ain't all I read! No commandant of Rurales would be crazy enough to put his name on a paper like that an' let you pack it across the Border!"

"*Quién sabe?*" The big Mex shrugged and spread his hands. "You ask, I tell. She's truth w'at is writ on them paper —" He broke off, body tense, head canted. The sound of hoofs came plain to all. With a muttered oath Kin Savvy snatched back his paper, hurriedly thrust it under his shirt; with his left hand scooped up his pistol, smoothly sheathed it and stood back against the wall, all the alert quick keenness swiftly ironed from his features. He looked, for that moment, all the world like some big oaf of a lead-witted peon.

Boots scraped the porch outside. The door burst open and with a rattle of spur chains Luce Jackman strode into the room. Other men peered in from the porch but Dane gave them no attention. There was a dark, urgent look in Luce Jackman's stare and he didn't take off his hat.

His glance flicked to Dane; fastened hard upon the girl. "Where's Jupe?" There was a violence in his words that drove the color from Dulcey's cheeks.

Her eyes clung frightenedly to his face as though she sensed he was the bearer of some news more dire than any thus far encompassed. She moistened her lips several times before she could make them voice her question. "What — what is it Luce? What has happened?"

"Nothing's happened yet, but Jupe has got to get out of here — pronto. Stroat's not five minutes back of me with a posse of twenty men!"

Dane said: "What's up, Jackman? What's —"

"Don't stand there asking questions," Jackman snapped. "Get him out of here! If that posse ever gets hold of him —"

"But Jupe's not here!" Dulcey cried. "He hasn't been —"

"Not here!" Luce Jackman's jaw sagged. "Not here?" he repeated ludicrously. "Why, I —" He broke off, growling angrily: "This is no time to bandy words. That posse —"

He let the rest trail off, staring fixedly at Kin Savvy. His cheeks took on a dark roan color; his eyes were narrowed, slitlike. A gray suspicion jumped to his stare. He appeared to forget his manners utterly. He said like a man bad treated, "Who the hell is this?" and stared resentfully from Dane to Dulcey; back again. "Who's this and what is he doing here?"

The hurried pound of larruping hoofs tore down on a stiffening wind.

But Dane said coolly, casually, "He's a fellow I just hired. He goes by the name of Kin Savvy —"

"*You* hired?" Jackman's cheeks went darkly red. "Who the hell gave you the right —"

"Perhaps you haven't heard," Dane said. "I'm roddin' this outfit, Jackman."

The man turned square around, turned angrily, accusingly. But Dulcey's nod gave him confirmation. She seemed confused, embarrassed, very conscious of their looks. But she said levelly: "Yes — he's looking after things for us till Jupe decides what we'd better do."

The sultry look left Jackman's cheeks. He got some kind of hold on himself. A wry sort of humor even touched his stare as he considered Telldane briefly. Then he shrugged. "You've picked a capable man, I guess; but I'm sorry you didn't consult me. Capability's all very well, but this is a time when — well . . ." He shrugged again, as though washing his hands of the business. "Consorting with fellows of this man's

92

stripe will not be improving Jupe's case any."

At the door he paused to look back at them. His glance, Dane thought, lingered longest on the round, moon face of the Mexican; and it was thoughtful, that glance — very thoughtful. "I'll try and get over some time tomorrow," he said, and went out, taking the men on the porch along with him.

They had not been gone two minutes when a second group of riders galloped into the yard. Boot heels hit dirt. Through the darkness and dust a shape strode toward the porch. His lifted voice came to them clearly. "Surround the place. Drop the first skunk that tries to get out of here." Then the speaker came in.

It was Alex Stroat, the sheriff.

7

Gun-Lashed Night

The edge of a bandage showed under his hat and the quick stab of his stare took on a malicious satisfaction when his sharpened glance swept across Telldane and, beyond Dane, big Kin Savvy. "Well!" he said with his stare squeezed thin; then, making out to ignore them: "No tricks now! Where's that brother of yours — that side-windin' killer, Jupe Dolton?"

Stroat's brutal question was flung at the girl, but it was Dane Telldane who answered. He said: "Mr. Dolton's not here."

"No? Well, I think different! An' you better keep your mouth plumb outa this! I ain't through with *you* by a long shot!"

He half turned then, and the glint of his stare rasped across the girl. He lifted his voice. "Come outa there, Dolton! You ain't got a chance! I got this shack plumb surrounded!"

But no Dolton came; and the sheriff's scowl darkened as it crossed Dane's grin. He seemed about to burst into speech. But with his mouth coming open for the air to back it, something he read in Dane's look stopped him. He moved his scowl to Dulcey.

He took his hat off gingerly, being careful to favor the place Dane had whacked with his gun barrel. "Nobody regrets this, ma'am, more than I do," he said, "but duty's duty an' I've had a tip Jupe's hid out here. Now let's avoid violence. You urge him to step out now an' give himself up like a gent—"

"He ain't here," Dane repeated. "And anyway, what proof you got he ever robbed those trains?"

"Trains!" the sheriff snorted. "I'm after Jupe Dolton for murder — wanton, cold-blooded murder! An' I'm —"

"But it's true! He's not here, sheriff — really! You've been misinformed!" Dulcey said in a strained, high key. Then, voice breaking: "Oh — why can't you *stop* this persecution? What has he done that you should hound him so? You'll *drive* him into being bad! You —"

"Beg pardon, ma'am, but nobody has to drive him. Jupe's plumb bad an' allus was — plumb ornery."

"That's a lie!" Dulcey screamed. "Jupe's —"

"Here, here!" Stroat growled. "No need to holler — I can understand your feelin' for him. Nobody blames you. But facts is facts. If Jupe didn't steal them cattle what'd he run for when I came to serve that warrant? If a man's on the square he's got nothin' to fear. Investigation'll clear him —"

Stroat caught Dane's grin and his cheeks took fire. "No matter!" he growled. "I've got Jupe dead to rights this time — got one of them gilt heels he sports — found it right there in the room! An' that ain't *all* I got! By grab, he'll swing —"

"But what's he *done?*" Dulcey cried.

"Done! I'll tell you — killed a woman; that's what he's done! Cut her all up and killed her!"

Dulcey Dolton stood stark. Rigid and breathless she stood, eyes horrified. Abruptly, uncontrollably, she screamed.

For a moment the men stood frozen. Then, curtly: "Stop that!" the sheriff snapped, starting toward her.

But Dane Telldane was there first. She was swaying, eyes glassy, when he caught her, eased her gently to a chair. Her arms fell across the table and she hid her face in them while shudder after shudder shook her.

96

Dane glared at Stroat and the lawman had the grace to flush while he fiddled with his hat embarrassedly. He would not meet the gun fighter's look. Self-consciously he wheeled and tramped the room for a turn or two while matters got no better. He scowled when his glance caught the weighing stares of the men he'd posted at the open door. He was a man of sound heart, but pigheaded. He'd had little experience in dealing with women. In red-faced consternation he blurted: "Uh — er — Gosh all hemlock, Miz Dulcey, ma'am! Don't be takin' on that way! I —"

"Don't make it worse. You've said enough," Dane growled. "If there's an ounce of decency in you, clear out an' —"

"I've got my duty to do," the sheriff said doggedly. "I've got a warrant —"

For a second, Dane's look swerved his thoughts; but Stroat's was a one-track mind and it was geared just now to law work. The dark blue serge of his store clothes snugged the angles of his shoulders as, with hands jammed hard in his pockets, his chin came up belligerently and he sent a snapped command to the possemen in the doorway. "Search the place!"

The deputies hesitated; but Stroat's scowl meant business and, reluctantly, the men came in and without enthusiasm set about it. It looked to be no mighty task. There was little space that would hide a man. The possemen peered under bunks, lackadaisically poked at blankets. While they were at it Stroat, staring hard at the sheeted figure in the farther one, asked hesitantly. "That Miz Dolton?"

Dane said, "You better look for yourself. A galoot suspicious as you are wouldn't take anyone's word for it anyhow."

But evidently Dane was wrong, for Stroat made no move to look under the covering; and his deputies, too, shied away from the chance of resting their eyes on a dead woman. "He ain't around here," one mumbled.

The sheriff, gingerly feeling his bandage, glared irritably at Dane. "It's uncommon odd," he muttered. "I'd of sworn he was hidin' out here."

Dane said nothing. The girl still sat with her face in her arms; and she did not speak, either.

Dane dropped a hand to her shoulder. She looked up listlessly with haggard cheeks. There was no hope in her brown-eyed stare. She looked at the sheriff dully.

Her regard increased his discomfort. He took a turn about the room with his hands still jammed in his pockets. When he came to Dane, Dane's dour glance stopped him, seemed to rowel up all his balked fury; or maybe it was remembrance of Dane's didos that blackened Stroat's scowl so bitterly. It seemed that he must surely choke, so darkly roan were his gaunt, set cheeks.

But he did not; he flung away, presently to pause beside the chair where Dulcey sat, staring beyond and through him. He seemed to want to say something; made two hard starts. Finally, gruffly, but not unkindly, he asked: "Would — would you be wantin' me to send the cor—"

"Jackman's sending Boswell out." Dane said it coldly, flatly.

"Eh? What's that? What's that — *Which* Jackman?"

"The young one — Luce, I guess he's called."

The sheriff stared. "When was — No matter! This is coroner's business now. I warn you not to move that body till the coroner's been an' looked at it. An' now I'll tend to *you!*" Stroat said. And the look his eyes slewed round at Dane promised full accounting for the things he held against him.

"Relieve that buck of his hardware!" he snapped. "An' get that greaser's, too. We're takin' 'em —"

"I guess not," Dane said. And the frozen quiet made a challenge of it.

The deputies stopped. They stared dubiously from Dane to the sheriff and back again. Something about the set of Dane's shape appeared to act as a brake, to fascinate them — that stance, even more than Dane's words, appearing to exude a singular influence. They stopped in their tracks and stood locked there.

"Not right now you ain't." Dane pushed his words at the sheriff. "You've got no case —"

"No case!" The sheriff snarled, "By Gawd —" and stopped. He'd mightly good reason for stopping. Dane's gun was out and squarely focused on the center of the lawman's vest.

"You was sayin' . . ." Dane drawled.

But Stroat was saying nothing. Not all the rage Dane had bottled in him could throw him from his caution then. He believed he read in Telldane's stare a gunfighter's lust to murder. The belief was unnerving. It shook him, clawed at him, pounded him. His face turned white as wood ash.

"Call off your outside crew," Dane said. "an' tell 'em to clear out. Tell 'em you're spendin' the night here; tell them anything you care to — but get 'em out of here. Fast-like."

The rage in Stroat was terrible but he dared not let it master him. He was convinced Dane would kill him without compunction; compelled by that knowledge he gave the order, and ere the sound of the posse's horses had died Dane told Kin Savvy to get Stroat's weapon, and the guns packed by his deputies.

It was a task the Mexican appeared to relish. With sly quips he felt them over; slapping leg, patting hip and shoulder. Not satisfied, he made them all pull off their boots. He hummed a ribald tune while they shook them. Then he looked at Dane and shrugged. There were four guns and a knife piled on the table. "I theenk mebbeso that ees all," he said.

"Throw 'em over on the bunk — that's fine. Now go out an' get their rifles. An' search their rolls an' saddlebags. When I pull fangs, I pull 'em."

The sheriff's bloated face was purple. He stood in apoplectic silence while Kin Savvy, returning, tossed three Winchesters on the bunk that held their pistols. Then, thick-choked with the fury riding him, the star packer gritted: "You'll rue this night! The both of you — an' Dolton, too, by

Gawd! If it takes the rest of my lifetime I'll see you all behind bars for this!"

Telldane's smile was gently skeptical. "Fair enough," he said. "While you're in the mood for talking, suppose you loosen up an' tell us who Jupe is accused of murderin'."

Stroat just glared. But one of the deputies obliged. "Sprawly Clark," he said, and Kin Savvy loosed a low whistle.

"*Caramba!* That Sprawly Clark, he's Black Jack's woman —"

"Ketchum's?"

"You bet!"

Telldane eyed the sheriff. Stroat nodded. With a feline glint of the teeth he said: "Thought he was right cute, I guess, but I been onto him quite a spell. Oh, yes — he's been makin' tracks around Sprawly now for goin' on a week. I been onto him, but he's been too slick to lay hands on. Been payin' her flyin' visits, an' she's been up in the hills with him, too —"

"Well, that's a goddam lie, anyway! She never has — *an' you know it!*"

The words came from the farther bunk — from the one with the sheet-covered figure. Only now the figure was upright, and above the folds of the tumbled sheet blazed the fierce blue eyes of Jupe Dolton.

The four men stared at him speechless. It would have been hard to say which was the more astounded, Dane Telldane or the sheriff.

Stroat's bloated cheeks were mottled. He was diving forward when Kin Savvy nabbed him. "Just a moment, meester!" He looked to Telldane for orders.

Dane growled at Jupe: "How'd you get here? I thought —"

"Never mind!" Jupe snarled, jumping off the bunk. Three strides took him to the sheriff. "You know damn well Sprawly never left town — you took good care that she shouldn't! Now what's this lie about me killin' her? I ain't even *seen* her for so much as a week — couldn't get within gunshot of her place! You been watchin' her like a cat —"

"I been watchin' her," Stroat said, "but you got by me —"

"Let's get this straight. Shut up a minute, Jupe. When was this woman killed?" Dane asked. "When'd you find her? Where?"

"We found her tonight — I had a deputy over there watchin' for him. Deputy come yellin' of a sudden some slinkin' son had killed her. I could see right off what happened. Place was a mess

— busted furniture strewed all over; an' there she was by the edge of her bed, blood all over an' with this crazy fool's knife stickin' out of her —"

"*My* knife!" Jupe cried. "Did you say *my* knife? I ain't never owned —"

"You can sling that bull at the jury, Dolton. They get paid to listen to it. *I ain't blind!* What's more, that knife ain't *all* we found. There was one of them fancy gilt heels of yourn kicked over under her writin' table!" Stroat's down-flashing glance took in Jupe's boots and a hard grin spread his lips. Changed 'em, have you? It'll take more'n that to save you! Every gent in this —"

He got that far when Jupe's fist struck him. Brought furiously up from his boot-straps, young Dolton's blow took Stroat in the teeth and smashed him backward three reeling steps with both hands clapped to his mouth.

Dane grabbed Jupe in a hammer lock, dragging him back, mad himself now. "Damn it, *quit!* Get over on that bunk an' stay there!" He shoved Jupe at it roughly. The sheriff was wiping blood from his lips and his eyes were like holes in a blanket.

"I'm sorry about that, Stroat," Dane said. "Jupe was a mite excited."

Stroat said nothing.

With a silent curse Dane took his arm. "Guess I'll ride with you after all."

Dulcey's stare was bewildered. Dane met Kin Savvy's look with a grin called up to deceive them. They must not guess how low were his hopes. "I'll be all right," he told them. "The Sheriff an' me, we're *amigos.*"

If they were, Stroat's look was a libel. But he took Dane's cue: moved toward the porch. Dane said, "Keep these deputies here. An' Jupe, you stay here with 'em."

He smiled at the girl, followed the sheriff out; but Dulcey came after him, clutching him.

"Dane!" He saw how the wind whipped her hair and skirt. In the lamp's yellow glow she looked panicky. "Dane!"

"Shucks! I'll be all right." He patted her shoulder, gently turned her back into the house. "Talk some sense into Jupe if you can. Keep him here; and remember — keep your chin up! I'll not be gone long."

He made it sound likely; yet coldly knew it was the most unlikely thing in the world he would ever see Dulcey Dolton again. But Stroat must be gotten away from here. Jupe was not to be trusted — not in that rage. He was being framed, and he knew it; and Dane Telldane knew it, too. Not by the sheriff necessarily, but . . .

He said to Stroat: "Has the body been moved?"

"Not if them fools obeyed orders. I've got two deputies guarding the place —"

"Men you can trust?"

Stroat snorted. He got into his saddle stiffly.

Dane swung into his own.

Through the night's deep black the Siding's lights flickered feebly. It was late, but a good many people still crowded the street. Dane said: "Don't try any foolishness."

The sheriff grunted. Wheeling left he bent a quarter-circle about the town, Dane riding close with his eyes peeled for trouble. The sheriff was a badgered man and there was no telling what fool play might appeal to him.

The dark outlines of a shack rose up and Stroat turned his horse toward it. Town lay behind, to the south of them now, and Stroat, pulling up, spoke into the shadows thick-piled about the shack. "This is it," he told Dane, and spoke again to the night, getting an answer this time. A vague shape moved through the murk, striding toward them and showing a glint of steel in the starlight. This shape stopped at the sheriff's stirrup.

"That you, Alex?"

Stroat said, "Had any trouble?" and Dane thought he placed more than necessary emphasis upon that final word.

The deputy appeared not to notice. "No trouble," he said. "Been several fellers prowlin' round here but we turned 'em back. Body's just like you left it — or ought to be. Ain't nobody been inside. You want in?"

Stroat said: "Keep your eye on these horses." Then, to Dane: "C'mon," he growled, and led the way inside.

The place was dark. Dane could hear Stroat fiddling with a lamp. A match scraped then and darkness fled. Dane noted the blanketed windows. His glance was jerked toward the bed.

This was a single-room shack. The bed was against the rear wall. Half on, half off it was a woman, the nightgown half torn off of her, one hand clutched into the bedclothes, the other dangling toward the floor. The rich dark mop of her tawny hair was tousled and tangled. Her lips were parted, disclosing teeth as lustrous as the rope of pearls that, across one creamy breast, hung floorward, throwing back the lamp's yellow light. The bold dark eyes were open, staring fixedly, dilated with horror.

She was dead. The knife hilt threw a black shadow across the pallor of her throat.

One raking glance showed Dane the room was just what the sheriff had called it — a mess. The shards of a mirror gleamed brittly from the worn straw matting on the floor. The matting itself was rumpled, a series of ripples like furrowed earth. A tintype glinted yonder from the wreckage of its frame. Knife-scarred, it was, those dents the result of the same blade, probably, that had ended the career of the woman. Leaning awry against the wall was a battered table, and Dane's eyes narrowed as he eyed the sole thing on it — the heel from a boot, long, bright-gilded.

Dane looked across at the sheriff. A sultry anger colored his glance.

"Like this — is that how you found it?"

"Except for the table and that boot heel. The table was overturned on the floor. The heel was underneath it."

Dane's smoky stare absorbed the rebellious detail of Alex Stroat's darkened cheeks. The man was ripe for violence. The least thing would touch him off.

Dane said: "Take it easy, Stroat. I know this has been pretty rough on you, but I'm here to help you if I can —"

"Of course you are," Stroat said; and Dane's vigilance heightened. "You've been helpin' me a lot."

Dane regarded him somberly. Shrugged. "Stand over there in that corner, Stroat. That's better. What give you the idea that knife belongs to Jupe?"

"Take a look at it."

"I'm goin' to," Dane said bleakly; "an' first move out of you I'll shoot."

He drew the six-shooter from his belt and crossed to the bed. Keeping one eye on the sheriff he took a quick squint at the handle of the blade that was buried in the woman's chest. Bone, it was, and burned with two initials — J. D. Jupe Dolton, they could stand for; but Jupe had said he'd never owned a knife. It would be un-common odd if he hadn't. Most cowmen packed one regularly for gotching steers' ears — this kind of one. But somehow Dane believed Jupe. At least he believed Jupe hadn't owned this one.

He could not say why this should be. Perhaps that shining thing on the table had more than a little to do with it. He knew Jupe owned a pair of gilt-heeled boots; a key to the man's vanity, those. Jupe had been wearing them that first night when Dane had met him — that night at the

Rafter line camp. But who would be fool enough to bury a marked knife in a woman and then leave a gilded heel behind to clinch the evidence against him? Not even *Jupe,* Dane felt, could be that rattleheaded.

No. Jupe was being framed; and the conviction made Dane surer than ever Jupe was not the fellow who was grabbing the Rock Island's pay rolls. Curiously, but with an eye fixed on the sheriff, he leaned forward and with his left hand pulled the covers from the arm the girl had on the bed.

The sheriff cursed, plain astounded. But Dane was neither surprised nor as startled as another man might have been by what his action revealed. Clenched in the girl's white fist — the hand that had been beneath those covers — was a man's hat. A crumpled, brown, flat-rimmed affair whose ownership Dane could guess.

"Dolton's?" he said.

Stroat started cursing. "You goddam butcher birds! This country'll never hold you after — Why, the bastard's *mad* — a crazy killer! We'll hunt him down like a wolf! An' *you* along with 'im! You'll never —"

"Never is a long time, Sheriff. I think —"

Dane ducked suddenly, twisting his body sideways. Stroat with a frantic leap had

110

smashed the lamp from its wall bracket and bright steel flashed in his hand. Swift stabs of flame leaped from that hand, ripping the howling darkness, pounding it with their thunder; and Dane felt the wind of those searching shots as he flung himself backward, rolled desperately.

Through the din Stroat slammed commands. "Watch 'im, boys! Don't let 'im get clear! *It's Telldane — he's tryin' for a getaway!*"

8

Realization

Railhead Frisby stepped quietly into Rolsem's back room and closed the door. There was a care and circumspection in the manner of his doing this, but it caught at Hake's attention, pulled his eyes up from the last month's *Tribune* he'd been slowly plodding his way through. He looked at Frisby and grunted.

"Well," he muttered, "what's up?"

Frisby dragged up a chair and sat there mulling it over. "This Dane Telldane —" he began at last.

But Rolsem checked him with an exasperated gesture. "Dane — *hell!*" he said explosively. "That's *Bufe,* I tell you! Don't I *know?* There ain't no Dane Telldane — that's Bufe! I've seen him forty times! D'you think anyone but Bufe would risk his neck to help a outlaw?" He mopped the sweat from his extra chins and glared at the Rock Island super. "I been over it time an' ag'in in my mind an' there's just one answer to it! The man is *Bufe* — every turn of his hand goes to prove it!"

There was a speculative light in Frisby's eye. He said, nodding: "I'd like mighty well to believe that, Hake; but, by cripes, I don't know. He looks awful young for a guy with Bufe's past — awful young." He said mildly: "You heard about last night, didn't you?"

"About him gettin' away from Stroat?" Rolsem nodded, wheezed an oath. "An' I say only Bufe could of cut it. Stroat had him bottled in Sprawly's shack, had two men outside coverin' it. I know them fellers — damn good shots. But the fool got away. I tell you, Rail, that guy is *Bufe!*" Rolsem pounded the desk for emphasis. "You might's well kiss your road goodbye. You'll never git a pay roll through — not with *him* helpin' Dolton."

Frisby snorted. "You ever hear of me quittin'? I never have, an' by God I'm too old to start now! Rock Island's goin' through to the coast —"

"Not with Telldane in the way of it —"

"Telldane won't be in the way of it *long,*" Frisby said; and Hake stared at him. "Telldane," the R.I. super said, "has just about reached the jump-off."

Rolsem took a cigar from his pocket and stuck it between his teeth. "That crack's got all the earmarks," he said derisively, "of somethin' from a half-wit." He put a match to the weed and, through its smoke, considered Frisby unfavorably. "It'll take somethin' a damned sight stronger'n cheap talk to kick that chunk off your rails."

Frisby smiled at him meagerly. "Quite so. We're agreed on that. Listen!" He hitched at his chair, leaned forward; spoke carefully, confidentially. Minutes passed. When he settled back in his chair again Hake Rolsem, the saloonman, whistled.

Telldane had got clear of Stroat's trap by a fluke. In ducking beneath Stroat's gunfire his hand had brushed a chair and, quick as light, he'd picked it up and smashed it through a window. Blanket, frame and all had gone; and through the startled cries of Stroat's outside men the sheriff's bull voice had shouted: "Get him! Goddam you — *stop him!*" Emptying his gun in the wake of the chair, Stroat had dashed to the window still spluttering oaths and orders. In the midnight murk the vague shape of the blanket-draped chair must have convinced the star packers they'd dropped him; and while the cagy deputies were pumping a final salvo into it to make doubly certain, Dane Telldane had found the door and quietly let himself out. By the time Stroat had realized the truth of things Telldane was away, riding hard.

But darkness and lack of familiarity with the landmarks had lost him good time. Though he did not know it, when at last he'd found the trail, there was a sheriff's posse ahead of him, and a raging Stroat was lashing it on with a flood of muleskinner invective.

All unaware of this, Dane quartered the night with his mind hard-probing its issues. Somebody certainly was out to frame Jupe, and the wild unthinking recklessness of Dolton's temper was playing right into their hands. Jupe's folly in striking Stroat had killed his last chance with the sheriff; from here on out, Quay County would hunt Jupe down unmercifully. The death of that woman would provide an incentive that heretofore had not been present to weight the scales against him. It could be only a matter of time until Jupe Dolton was run to earth — perhaps killed.

And the man was innocent. At least Jupe had not killed Sprawly Clark. No matter what motives were lugged from the obscurity of forgotten happenings to clinch the case against him, Jupe Dolton, Dane was convinced, had not been guilty of that killing.

Oh, his was the unstable temper, the reckless anger — perhaps the need. Jupe, under given circumstances, might well have done a thing like that; might well have roused to the killing rage it would take to slit a woman's gullet. But Jupe had not slit Sprawly Clark's! Not even *he* could be such a fool as those dropped clues must prove him! No man — Dane felt this keenly — could be so crazy, killing mad as to leave with his victim a marked knife, a known hat, and a thing conspicuous as that boot heel!

He might have left one. Any man might in the sudden repentance of violence. The engulfing remorse, the sudden horror of his deed, the acute fear of swift reprisal — these: any one of them, might make a man forget *some*thing. But not under any circumstance could a man have forgotten all three.

Logic urged this conclusion on Dane; the same logic that had weighed one other thing — the arrangement of the woman's pearls. They had sloped down from her neck to lie across that round, exposed breast, from there to dangle movelessly beside the arm stretched toward the floor. The stage had been well set but for this and for that superabundance of clues. But

116

this was a fact that could not be blinked; once seen it had to be recognized, and all it implied must be considered. The dead woman lay in a room abounding with signs of violence. Things shouting "Fight!" had strewn that place — marks of struggle, of murder made difficult. Was it conceivable that a rope of pearls had come through such a fracas unbroken? *Unbroken round the dead woman's neck?*

It was three-fifteen when Dane reached the ranch. The place seemed deserted. The line camp shack's gaunt angles drearily leered at him through the gloom. The wind had died to a dismal moaning, a low whimpering foaled by the oak brush.

What had happened? Where were they, the three men he'd left with Dulcey? The corral stood empty, its bleached poles standing askew and bare like the bones of departed buffalo. The horses were gone. A door hinge screaked and Dane sprang from the saddle, went stiff as a sharp command jumped the murk.

"Don't move!"

Then his breath came out with a vast relief as he recognized Dulcey's voice. "It's me," he called softly; and Dulcey cried, "Dane!" and ran to him. She held him tightly with her face hard-pressed to his chest.

"Dane! Oh, Dane, they'll *catch* him! Jupe will never be free again! They're hunting him now — they've got blood-hounds. *Listen!* You can hear them baying!"

Dane heard. Far off they were and faint, but unmistakable.

He could feel the trembling of her body and he patted her shoulder, manlike, trying to soothe her but finding no words.

She said huskily, "Everything I've ever loved is gone . . . But I don't care. It — it don't seem to matter, now you're back. Do what you will with me, but don't leave me, Dane —" She caught her breath, threw her head back, face tilted up to him. "Don't leave me — *ever.*"

And suddenly she was crying. And Dane shut his eyes and held her, and his jaws were locked like granite.

9

Trapped!

A sudden, low mutter of hoof sound pulled them apart. A pair of hard-ridden horses broke from the trees, larruped into the yard and went back on their haunches, hauled up by rough tugs of the bits.

"*Quién es? Quién es* — who is it?"

It was the Mex, Kin Savvy, with a shotgun flung to his shoulder. The man with him was Dolton; and a six-shooter glinted from each of his hands.

It was a hair-triggered second; and then Dane said: "It's me, you fools! What're you doing here? What the hell's happened?" And the girl jumped across to catch Dolton's hands, to hug them to her fearfully, clutched tight against her breasts. They spoke to each other: low, whispered words that were lost in Kin Savvy's answer.

"*Caramba!* Eet is them dogs! By Christ, she's bark all over country. We hear them coming — we was wait here like you say — an' Jupe, she's say, 'Come on — Jeez Chris' we got to get outa here!' An' off we went like a wind in the crick — *pues,* yes! You nevair see such ridin'! But them dogs, she's hard to shake; an' we come back, for see eef you here —"

"Who was with those dogs? Not Stroat?"

"Jeez Chris' eet was! I hear hees voice — all the time raise hell weeth posse. I'm think, by Jeez —"

But Dane wasn't listening. Evidently the sheriff had known some short cut — had guessed Dane would make for the ranch. The man would be hog-wild to get them: Jupe for the murder of Sprawly Clark, and Dane for the loss of his dignity — for making him look like a muttonhead.

No rest for weary bones this night. They'd have to ride, and ride pronto!

"Jupe! Kin Savvy! How are them broncs — will they last the night, do you reckon?"

The boys said yes; and Dane reached for the horn, was lifting a boot to the stirrup. But Dulcey saw. She flew to Telldane; clutched his arm, voice desperate. "You can't leave me! Dane — My God! Don't leave me — *please!*"

Dane stared down at her, moveless, held by the look in her eyes.

"We got no time for girls tonight," Jupe snarled, in a sweat to be gone. "Leave go of him, Dulcey — you'll be all right. Nobody'll —"

But they weren't heeding. Dane took his boot from the stirrup; stepped down. He took the girl by the shoulders, looked searchingly into her face. Then he nodded, lifted her into the saddle. He stood there a moment, listening. Then he swung up behind her, "Come on."

Jupe swore. Harsh words blazed out of him — angry ones. Words that showed how the lone trails had shaped him; what the hounding of posses had done to him. He was a lobo. Escape was all he could think of. He was what the law had made of him.

Dane listened without interruption. When the man was done he said, "She's going with us," and knew what chance, what risk, the decision invited. He repeated it. "Dulcey goes with us. Lead off. By the sound, Stroat's getting close."

"*Caramba,* yes!" Kin Savvy cried, and jabbed the steel into his pony.

When the posse burst into the clearing the place was empty, deserted, abandoned. Stroat, breathing blasphemies, strode through the house like a cyclone; came stamping back out on the porch. "Let's have a light there — *you!* Hold onto them dogs! Strike a match, Kurt, an' look for tracks. I know the dogs'll find 'em — I want to look at 'em with my *own* eyes. I got a notion. . . ." He broke off, went back into the house.

When he came out Kurt, the reticent first deputy, beckoned him. Striking a match he held it low above the ground at a point near the edge of the oak brush. The sheriff took a look and nodded.

"They've grabbed up their things an' cut for it. They'll not come back," he said bitterly. "They're takin' it on the run. By God, we've got our work cut out — but we'll get 'em! We'll get 'em, an' don't you forget it!" He stared out across the blackness. "I know every inch of these mountains; I know the damn deserts blindfold. An' I tell you by God we'll get 'em! Turn loose them dogs!"

Dane held their pace to an easy jog. From time to time the distant baying of Stroat's hounds came to them, causing the girl to shiver and bringing from Jupe impatient curses and dire predictions. But Telldane would not be hurried.

"Let 'em bark," he told Jupe gruffly. "It ain't the thunder that hurts you. We may need these broncs for a right good while an' I don't propose to founder 'em. Let Stroat run the hocks off his horses; time enough to run when he sights us —"

"Yeah? An' what about when dawn comes?" Jupe snarled. "What about that, eh? He'll have us right where he wants us. If we don't run now we'll never git clear. Come day, we'll show like a bonfire an' —"

"Let's worry about that when day comes," Dane said dryly. "Your job right now is to circle back some way and get us up into the Sierra —"

"*Pues*, wait!" Kin Savvy muttered. "The sheriff, she'll look in them mountains sure. *Seguro;* let heem look there. You fin' them Bonito Crick an' make like we aim for Canadian. Them dogs no can trail through water. W'en we hit thees creek we turn south — sabe? Through the brakes an' up back of Cap Rock —"

"Too settled! Too many towns!" Jupe snarled. "Why, they'd have us 'fore you can —"

"Just a minute," Dane said. And to Kin Savvy: "After we get back of Cap Rock — what then? You know some place we can fort up? Some place where Stroat won't find us?"

The Mexican shook his head, but his teeth gleamed in the starlight. "Them

Sheriff, she's know thees country like the book. Hees star, she's no good down yonder."

"You mean . . . Curry County!" Dane said. And Kin Savvy chuckled.

Dane thought it over. Stroat might be fooled and head north when his dogs lost the scent, or he might not. But even should Stroat guess the truth they'd be no worse off than at present. It was worth a try; once let them get out of Quay County, the law's machinery would bog down.

It would be better, he thought, to split up now, go separate ways and rejoin at Pleano. This would slow pursuit, confuse the issue; it would hamper Stroat's tracking and scatter his posse. There was merit in the plan but Dane discarded it. To follow it would compromise Dulcey, and he'd not do that, come what might.

He said: "O.K., Jupe. Head for the Bonito and shake it up all you've a mind to."

Unless they reached the stream with Stroat beyond hearing, he would know which way they turned. With this knowledge he could race along the bank, outdistance them and cut them off — could wait for them in ambush. There was chance any way a man might look. But the horses would have to take it now. Speed had become essential, and till they reached the creek it must remain the prime requisite to safety.

As they rode he slowly drew from the girl the story of what had happened. Shortly after he'd set out for town — in the morning that was — Hame Boswell had come for Mrs. Dolton's body and had taken it away in his wagon. That had been a break for Jupe; he'd reached the ranch not half an hour after Boswell's departure. He'd been there when Kin Savvy had come; had stayed in the house under cover. Kin Savvy had told the girl that Dane had sent him; that he would hide in the brush and keep an eye on things till Dane got back. Both Dulcey and Jupe had recognized him instantly as one of the men who had been with Ketchum when Ketchum had come hunting Jupe; and neither one thought of believing him. Both suspected he was there by Ketchum's orders — sent over to watch for Jupe. Jupe had wanted to slip away but Dulcey had been afraid to let him: there might be more Ketchum men hid out in the brush. She'd persuaded Jupe to wait for Dane.

And then Dane had come, though later than expected. Not knowing in night's darkness whether it was Dane or one of the sheriff's deputies, Jupe had made haste to crawl into the bunk and Dulcey in an access of fear had pulled the sheet up over him. And there he'd stayed while Dane called in Kin Savvy; and, before Jupe could make his presence known Luce Jackman had come and Jupe, grown overcautious now, had decided to stay where he was. He must have sweat blood after Jackman left and Stroat with his scalp-hunting posse rode in.

"But it was too late for him to get away then," Dulcey said. "I was panic-stricken when Alex told those two men to start searching."

"You did a mighty fine bit of acting," Dane told her warmly. "Too bad Jupe didn't have the wit to stay hid out. Jumpin' up that way an' plantin' his fist in the sheriff's face hasn't improved his case with Stroat any." He shrugged a thought away. "Shucks, the fat's in the fire now an' talk ain't goin' to change it any. You're a mighty brave girl, Dulcey Dolton."

A silence closed. Each let it ride, engrossed in personal thinking. Through the chipping sound of pony hoofs, through the creak and jingle of saddle gear, Dane said: "Kin Savvy — what happened to those two posse men after I left with Stroat?"

Kin Savvy said over his shoulder: "Them fellers? She's tie up out in the brush. Be fin' tomorrow sure."

"After Jupe and him came back," Dulcey said, "Jupe made bold to laugh at the idea of Kin Savvy being a Rurale, they had it back and forth hot and heavy, Jupe claiming he was a sneaking Ketchum spy and —"

Jupe called back just then to say they had reached the Bonito. "You want I should head south now?"

"No. Swing north and ride in the creek bed. I want Stroat to figure we're heading for Logan or Lokna."

They heard Jupe splash in, heard Kin Savvy follow. Then Dane swung his own horse in and cold water tugged at his boots. The creek right here was eight feet wide and belly-high to their horses.

"That's far enough," he called to the others. "Turn around an' we'll follow it south."

Dane and the girl now had the lead, and all went well till suddenly, malignantly, above the horses' splashing, Jupe Dolton swore and Kin Savvy snarled: "Jeez Chris'! *Cuidado, hombre* — watch out who you're shove!"

"You slat-sided spy!" Jupe shouted. "You pulled that trick on pur—"

"What's up back there?" Dane demanded. "You want to tell Stroat where we're at?"

Jupe's growled answer implied that was what Kin Savvy'd been up to.

"Like the hell! Theese damfool hombre poosh me!"

Getting a grip on his temper Dane rode back to where the two men sat their horses, each trying to outglare the other. "Let's hear it," he said. "What's the matter?"

"Damn sneakin' greaser had his bronc out on the bank back there! He's leavin' sign for Stroat to follow!" Jupe blazed wrathfully.

"Is goddam lie! He poosh me!" the big Mex cried. "He crowd me weeth hees caballo!"

Dane eyed the fellow narrowly. He wasn't sure about Kin Savvy yet. The man appeared sincere; but there was still that unexplained business about the paper he packed inside his shirt with a seal and a man's name signed to it. And Dane could not forget this fellow had worked for Jack Ketchum — might be working for him now.

But the harm was done. They'd no time now to search for tracks; no time to be rubbing them out. Speed was all that could count for them now. With Jupe and Kin Savvy at dagger point there was no use in leaning on stealth; no chance in it for them longer.

"Never mind," Dane said; "we'll talk of that later. C'mon — we're leavin' the creek!"

A single-file trail ran along the left bank and Dane swung the big roan into it. Jupe growled at Kin Savvy with a cold, brash violence, "You next, hombre — you're not goin' to leave any more billy-doos," and held his horse back till Kin Savvy went past. Then he swung in behind, alert for a trick, with a pistol gripped in each fist.

Dane increased the pace but kept it short of a gallop; galloping hoofs could be heard a long way and it was not Dane's intention to help Stroat more than necessary. He rode with one hand loosely gripping the horn, and the way the girl lay against his arm any other time would have been an experience to remember; but right now his mind was too taken up with the grim realities of this ride to be giving much thought to romance. For the life of him he could not make up his mind which side Kin Savvy was backing. Was he sincere in claiming he'd cut loose of Ketchum? Was that gunplay in town the real thing, or had it been staged to foist the Mex onto them?

He wanted to believe in Kin Savvy. The fellow was a likable hombre; a kind of rough diamond and powerful fast with his shooting iron. But that paper he had shown them — Dane's mind always harked back to that. It didn't stand to reason that any commandant of Rurales — Mex military police — would be such an addlepated fool as to sign any document intended to be carried by a subordinate across the Border into Yankeeland. Men had been sent north before on a mission, just as sometimes Rangers took a pasear south; but such agents were men beyond the pale, men dependent on their wits — free lances, unowned, without claim on their homeland. Dane hadn't read Kin Savvy's paper — more than to glance at the seal and signature. No agent of a foreign government bound on a secret mission ever rode with papers to prove it.

Uncommon odd, the whole business; inscrutable as the man. With a baffled, uneasy shake of the head Dane put the thing out of mind for the moment. The main job right now was to shake off pursuit, and he bent to the task all his energies.

He would not think of Dulcey as in any way a handicap. But he knew very well Old

Frosty, his roan, could not long maintain so fast a lope overburdened as he was by two riders. Something must be done, and quick, some strategy thought of, or they'd find themselves snared — at the least, engaged in a gun battle. For already Stroat's riders must have reached the creek — had perhaps picked up their sign again. Or they would mighty soon. That was certain. Those dogs —

"Into the creek again!" he ordered; and the spray splashed up in his face as the roan's chest breasted the water. The creek was deeper here and they made slow work of it. So slow in fact that five minutes later Dane ordered them out. "We'll try the other bank for a while."

But that, too, was slow and hard work; for there was no trail on this side and the thorny growth clutched at them, scratched them. "Back into the creek!" Dane growled with an oath, and for another ten minutes they fought it. Then back onto the trail Dane kneed the big roan, satisfied that if Stroat's posse were still on their track, good time must be lost here finding it. Not even bloodhounds could trail through water; they would have no quarter for sign again.

Then far to their rear he heard the dogs bay.

131

Stroat's crew had reached the creek.

Against his chest, in the circle of his arm, he felt Jupe's sister tremble. He put his mouth to her ear, made an effort to re-assure her. "Don't worry," he said. "They're a long way back — they'll be losing the sign in a minute."

But his words proved optimistic. The barking continued, came hurrying on. Dane called a halt to make sure. Tense in their saddles they listened, heads canted; and abruptly Jupe Dolton swore.

"By God, they're comin' straight on!" he snarled, and glared at Kin Savvy malevolently. "I've a damn good notion —"

"That's enough of that! Put up that gun!" Dane snapped. "I'm bossin' this, an' you'll take my orders or play your string out solo!"

Jupe muttered under his breath, but he put his gun up finally. "O.K.," he sneered. "Keep trustin' this Spik if you want to end up on a tree limb. For two cents I'd *play* it alone —"

"Jupe!" Dulcey cried. "Don't talk that way! Dane's doing his best to help us. The least we can do is —"

"O.K., O.K.," Jupe said testily. "Never mind the sermon."

Dane scowled in the dark; gathered up

his reins. To Kin Savvy he said curtly: "If you know any short cuts, hombre, take the lead an' let's get out of this."

Without a word the man swung off and they fell in behind him silently. He drove a right angle through the thick brush and Dane felt the girl flinch from its needles. But she locked her lips, never uttered a cry, and soon they were out in the open. The creek fell behind, and the trail and the brush; and a long flat opened before them, pale, vague-gleaming in the light of the stars. Sand! They were out on the desert.

He saw the flash of Kin Savvy's big spurs. Their horses stretched into a run. "We make for them black line off there," the Mexican called. And following the sweep of his hand Dane saw, low-crouched in the distance, what looked like the rim of a long chain of hills.

"Cap Rock!" the girl cried softly.

"How far?"

Across hunched shoulder the Mex called back: "Mebbeso feefteen mile."

They seemed to be cutting a circle now, a wide arc whose end lay somewhere in those yonder hills. To their right, perhaps five miles away, a dark butte rose and Dulcey, sensing his interest, said: "Mesa Redonda. We're heading into broken country. I think he's heading for Puerto —"

"Is there a pass through there?"

"Just south of there. The bed of a creek — it's a dry wash now. Through the bluffs of the Llano Estacado. We're on the llano now."

Dane said: "What do you suppose made Jackman think Jupe was at the ranch tonight?"

Jupe heard his words, and before Dulcey could answer he threw out a question of his own: "Where the hell did Stroat get his information?" And Dane saw him twist his head and stare at big Kin Savvy. "Somebody tipped him off, an' I'm bettin' I could hit the guy with a rock right now!"

Kin Savvy twisted in the saddle. "Me, I'm bet thees Luce Jackman, she 'ave been watch your place weeth glasses."

Jupe snorted. But Dane was not so certain but the Mexican had hit on something. Jackman had known, all right. And now that Dane stopped to think on it, he found something uncomfortably suspicious in the Square & Compass foreman's actions. The man had appeared astounded at not finding Jupe there. He'd seemed to think they were lying to him; and Jupe really *had* been there. Unless Kin Savvy were right, how had Jackman known it?

Indeed, how had the *sheriff* known it?

More and more they were bearing east and the bluffs were drawing closer. It was cool on this high desert with a downdraft shoved from the hills. A changeless land, dark, somber, silent with the hush of centuries; a forlorn and dismal country where anything might happen — where a lot of things probably *had* happened.

The reflection whipped up his vigilance. Peering ahead, beyond the bobbing of the Mexican's big Chihuahua hat, he saw the girl had been right. This was a broken terrain they were riding into, a region of up-and-down draws and eroded gullies, a crazy maze of canyons twisting into the tumbled hills.

The upthrust heights of sheer rock walls rubbed out the thin light of the stars, and suddenly they were traveling through the solid dark, feeling their way, seeing not a thing before them. Somewhere in the black above, a shooting star scratched a luminous streak across the dying night, and a wind off the cliffs brought down the far sound of dogs barking.

Perhaps he had been brash in letting Kin Savvy map their course; possibly he should have paid more heed to Dolton's words. After all, what did they know of the man

save that he had been in Ketchum's pay —
and still might be? For himself Dane could
take his chance, but it angered him to
think that by his act he perhaps had placed
Dulcey's life at the doubtful mercy of a
tricky Ketchum spy. The thought kicked
violence through him and snapped his
hand half down to the open-topped holster
that rode the gun on his hip. The hand
started down, but before it touched leather
he stiffened, snapped bolt upright behind
Jupe's sister; felt her body tensing, too.

"What was that?" he cried. "Hold on!"

But he knew — they all knew. A horse
had nickered. Plainly. Close. The sound of
it unmistakable. They were trapped!

Dane's narrowed stare raked the gloom
ahead. He saw the outline of Kin Savvy's
hat drop suddenly as with a ripped-out
curse Jupe twisted in the saddle. Three
times flame threw its lurid light from his
hip toward where the Mexican had
dropped from sight; then gunfire split the
night wide open.

10

"Step Out of That Saddle!"

Trapped!

Dane realized it bitterly; saw in a flash what had probably happened. Stroat had split his posse and, some way, part of it had got ahead, was here before them, holding this wash, blocking them, dug in to keep them till the rest of Stroat's men with the dogs came up!

There could not be more than one answer to that. The Mexican, Kin Savvy, had played them false; had tipped Stroat off or was a plant from the first, deliberately leading them into this ambush!

It made Dane boil. But even with that fury rioting through him he could not forget Jupe's sister. They must get her clear! Some way he and Jupe must manage to —

He thrust dry lips close against her ear as he flung the big horse round in its tracks. He shoved the reins in her hands. "Ride — an' ride fast!"

She had no time to argue. Dane slid

clear, slashed his hat hard against the bronc's rump and whirled, gun in hand, to face the unseen posse men whose gun flames stabbed the gulch's deep murk.

He heard Jupe cursing. He was twenty feet to the left trying to curb the pitching of his terrified horse. "Get down!" Dane shouted. "Get out of the saddle!" But he knew the sound of his words was lost. Gun thunder slammed the canyon walls, and through that turbulence nothing could be heard but the scream of lead and the *crack-crack-crack* of high-powered rifles.

Yet Jupe got down. He must have sensed the target he made high and black against the stars. The wonder was that he had the chance. But perhaps the antics of his frenzied mount had saved him — perhaps he hadn't been born to die that way. Dane wished he could be sure *he* hadn't!

The yellows and mauves of muzzle light flashed clear across the wash's cluttered bed, ringed it, faintly looming the rocks that sheltered the posse. Dane dropped behind a boulder and found Jupe already there, one hand still clamping the reins of his bronc.

"Cut loose!" Dane growled. "Can't you hear him thrashing? That horse'll never take you another step!"

Jupe seemed to have forgotten he had hold of the reins. He hurled them away. With his twisted face shoved close to Dane's: "Where's that bastard Mex? Tell me! By God, I'll —"

Dane said: "Where's your rifle?"

"On the horse —"

Dane left, wriggling backward, every nerve screaming protest at such reckless exposure. The trip was a nightmare. The horse was dead. Dane's reaching hand touched the rifle. But he could not budge it — it was under the horse. He worked back to Jupe; found him wasting lead crazily, the savage fury that had hold of him squeezing his trigger each time a gun flashed.

"Try usin' your head!" Dane gritted. "You're throwin' that lead at the law!"

"Law, hell! That's *Ketchum's* outfit! Morg Trotter's out there — McGinnis, too! I saw 'em!"

"You got damn good eyes then," Dane chucked back at him, but did not doubt Jupe. He remembered what the Ketchum boss had told him — that his hand would be called if he stuck around. He thought of the man who had been with Morg Trotter and his eyes got bleak and narrow. Flat as the prairie miles was the voice that shoved the next words out of him. "Load up. We're goin' to make Morg sick."

Bent low behind the rock's protection they fumbled fresh shells to their emptied pistols, each man loading an extra gun and keeping it by him, ready. Dane said, "Stick here; I'll do my bit from the other end. Count ten an' pick the farthest flash to the left; then drop an' count ten again. We'll empty a few of those hats out there."

He was just sliding into position when Jupe opened up. Dane let that first one go. When the next came he was ready. The rifleman Jupe had sniped at came up for another try and Dane tagged him. They could hear his scream above the shot's sound. Dane said cold as bell steel, "Pick another one, Dolton." But Jupe wasn't picking anything.

Lead pounded their shelter with the rattle of hail, only louder and considerably more vicious. Twigs dropped from an overhead tree and Jupe alternately cursed and grunted as he dug the hot sand with his belly.

Something had to be done, and done quick. They might duck out of this by retreating — but that was the one thing Dane wouldn't do. Sooner would he have cut off an arm than drag this battle after

Dulcey. Stroat would be warned and, deploying his men, must surely catch her. Dane had sent her away out of fear for her safety, and he didn't want Stroat stopping her. Not that the sheriff would treat her roughly; but, crook or honest forthright lawman, Stroat was in a temper now that would not scruple at using her to further his ends. He might hold her as hostage or use her for bait to lure Jupe into some tighter trap; and Dane knew well that once the law had got him Jupe was done for. Good men had been killed in those train robbings and — there was Sprawly Clark. Men wouldn't worry overmuch concerning the end of a woman killer.

Jupe snarled: "We better run for it! Those birds are gettin' set to rush —"

"Wait!" Dane, lifting forward on hands and a knee, leaned cautiously outward. "Work your gun," he grunted, "while I take a look."

Jupe emptied his pistol without sighting. Dane had his quick squint but it did not add much to their knowledge. The gulch was too dark for observation and each flash of the Ketchum rifles but left the returned gloom deeper. A three-quarters moon was creeping up, but a high wind off the mesa was keeping the cloud banks rolling and Dane prayed fervently they would keep on rolling until he and Jupe cut loose of this.

But that was the joker — how to *get* loose!

Jupe crawled over. "We better move quick —"

Dane's jaws clamped as the sound of baying hounds crossed a slack in the Ketchum firing. Stroat was getting close; intermittently they could catch the muffled hoofbeat of his horses. He was placing all bets on bottling them up. With the backtrail locked he could force surrender; and that was what he was up to.

Dane felt Jupe's gaze scratch across him. Their situation was getting no better. With a sudden grunt Jupe turned; inching back, he crawled for a high spot where a fault in the rock held the promise of a better vantage. His gun cracked suddenly, savagely, and out there in the creek bed somebody cursed.

"Trotter," Jupe muttered. "I hope to hell I nicked him!" He twisted his neck around. "Your gun shot dry?"

Dane said: "I'm thinkin'." And he was — thinking hard; but it wasn't helping.

He wondered: "How would Bufe be handlin' this?" And suddenly, almost regretfully, he knew what they had to do.

"Jupe!"

"Comin'." Dolton's shape slid down to him. Jupe blew on his knuckles. "I'd like to get my hands on that sneakin' —"

"Por Dios! On me?" a voice drawled right at their elbows.

Dane lunged, grabbing Jupe. He got a hold on Jupe's gun hand. Backward, forward they swayed in a wild and panting struggle, Jupe striving to fire, Dane's strength taxed to the utmost in the effort he put forth to stop him. But he won; got Jupe's fist down and held it there.

Kin Savvy said: "Jeez Chris' — I swear she's like for keel me!"

"You can count me in on that like too! There's a score —"

"Válgame Dios!" the big Mex growled, and his voice to Dane seemed entirely earnest. "You theenk I'm done these theeng on purpose? *Carajo!* You forget that fight at corral? You theenk they're like me more tonight — eh? By gar, I'm tell you them Black Jack she's no forget —"

"Me, neither! Get goin'," Dane advised him.

But Kin Savvy would not have it that way. He said, "I'm thought we was *buen amigos* —"

143

"*Was* is the right word, fellow! I —"
Dane broke off, panting.

Jupe was cursing, twisting again, striving
to get his gun up. He was like an eel. It was
all Dane could do to hold him. And suddenly he was loose, slipped out of Dane's
clutch, panting, glaring wickedly into the
dark about them. But the Mex was gone,
slipped away like a shadow; and the growl
of Jupe's words held bitterest fury.

"You crazy fool! I —"

"Stow it! We got to cut an' run for it. We
got to keep this fight on the move — keep
it noisy, or Stroat'll be gettin' his claws on
Dulcey —"

"Dulcey!" Jupe caught Dane by the
throat. "God damn your white-livered
soul! Where is she?" he screeched. *"Where
is she?"*

Dane broke his hold. A jarring, teeth-
jolting left to the chin set Jupe back on his
heels, arms flailing. Dane gave him another. Jupe dropped, spread-eagled, hung
up in his spurs.

When he got himself collected, was getting shakily to his feet, Dane said: "Get
this, an' get it straight! There's just one
boss on this job an' that's *me!* You can take
it that way or play it solo. This was no
damn time to be jumpin' Kin Savvy. As for

your sister — she's gone on my horse to get out of these bullets. This ain't no pink tea an' it's goin' to be less so. Now — you backin' my play or stiff-neckin' your own boat?"

In the darkness he could feel Jupe's glare. Before the man could speak or Dane could press him, a wild halloo echoed up the back trail and Ketchum's men set up a shout. "Get 'em, boys!" came a bull-throated bellow. Boot clatter thumped the night and the rock walls rang to the Ketchum charge.

Dane flung his torso clear around in a cat-quick jump that poised him tensely. He dragged the extra gun from under his armpit. With an iron in each fist his glance raked the rock tops. A man's head loomed through the swirling murk; Dane put two slugs just below it.

Hat and head both dropped on the instant. Then back of them Stroat's hoarse shout called Ketchum. "Hold 'em, Jack! Don't let 'em get by you! We're comin' —"

The crash of Jupe's pistol drowned the rest; and all was confusion, dust and hurtling bodies dim-seen through a gloom that was knifed by red gun flame.

"Quick! This way!" Dane cried, catching hold of Jupe's shoulder. "Flat on the ground — an' keep your gun silent!"

Inch by inch like snakes in the sand they wriggled through the maze of upthrust boulders, crawling for the gulch side where muzzle light had seconds earlier shown a fissure in the sandstone walls. Snail-slow they crawled; and with the salt sweat dripping from his chin Dane prayed the lopsided moon would stay hid a bit longer — would stay back of the cloud that, above the left-hand rim, was like a charcoal smudge on a rain-drenched potlid.

Above them, all about them among the rocks and churning the sand of the creek's dry bed, swarmed Stroat's possemen and Ketchum's riders, cursing, shouting, firing wildly at shadows and damning one another for goggle-eyed fools. Stroat's raging voice slammed the rock walls madly. "Ketchum! Goddam you, where are you? Trotter! Luke — where the hell's that greaser?"

"Light a fire, you clowns!" Ketchum bellowed. "Light a blaze before they get away!"

"Fire! Blaze!" Stroat snorted. "With *what?* The tail off a comet? You drunken fool! Them birds have got by you! What're you —"

"They never got by *me!*" Ketchum snarled.

Stroat jumped his horse across Dane without seeing him. He cursed Ketchum raggedly.

"If you'd been onto your job," Ketchum lashed, "we'd have got the both of 'em!" Rage threatened to strangle him. "They never got by *me*! If they've skipped, blame yourself!"

Morgan Trotter threw in: "If we had a man packin' the tin 'stead of a damn' ol' woman —"

"Come on — come on!" Stroat snarled at them thickly. "Jawin' around ain't doin' no good! We'll shove through the pass an' —"

"You can shove by yourself," Ketchum said. "I'm through!"

Dane dragged Jupe into the fissure. Jupe was wounded, unconscious — bad hurt by the look. Dane couldn't be sure without making a light; and he dared not risk that. Ketchum had gone — had taken his riders; but Stroat was still beating the gulch down below them with half of his posse. The rest he'd sent through the pass, off toward Pleano, still doggedly certain his quarry had gotten past Ketchum.

The wind increased, running the gulch with an eerie whistling. The moon had come clear, tangled up with more clouds.

147

Deep back in the fissure Dane dragged young Dolton, then sat on his boot heels, filled with aches and miserable, too tired to think — to sleep; content just to crouch there and sweatily shiver. With no thinking left in him, chin wedged on chest, he hunkered there above the out-sprawled form of Jupe Dolton. Sometimes Jupe moaned a little or mumbled some incoherent phrase that Dane in his weariness disregarded.

But with the false dawn's light Dane roused himself. Creeping to the lip of their tortuous cranny, his haggard stare found the gulch empty. Stroat's posse was gone; and the dead and the wounded. Perhaps none had been dead; but Dane knew there were wounded — the fellow Jupe dropped, those he'd winged himself. "And if Ketchum an' Stroat's crowd didn't blast hell out of each other the devil must have been looking' after 'em uncommon well!" he muttered.

Staring, he went suddenly stiff. Head canted, he crouched listening while a hand slid swiftly hipward. Round a bend in the canyon wall came a horseman, a solitary rider jogging slowly forward, alert gaze casting for sign in the trail before him. A vaquero-garbed man that, with a curse, Dane knew for Kin Savvy.

The Mexican came on, bent low in the saddle as he scanned the trail.

Two buzzards left their roost on fresh horse meat, departing the place with a great flapping of wings.

Kin Savvy crossed and recrossed the creek bed several times before, abruptly, he wheeled his bronc and came straight toward Dane's hide-out.

Gun in hand Dane straightened.

"That's far enough," he said softly. "Step out of that saddle!"

11

Peace Pact

If Kin Savvy felt surprise he did not show it. He grinned up at Dane widely and, pulling up his sleeves to show he had no gun cached there, climbed lazily from the saddle and leaned against his horse. Lounging there, grinning blandly and very evidently not at all embarrassed, he one-handedly rolled a smoke, snapped a match to flame on a thumbnail. "*Buenos dias, señor.* She's damn' fine morning, no?"

"It's a good enough day for a killin'," Dane said. "Hang your gunbelt on the saddle horn an' step this way. Step careful."

Kin Savvy consideringly rasped his jaw, eyed Dane and shrugged. With the languor of a true caballero he unbuckled his belt and leisurely hung it, pistol-weighted, to his saddle. He turned then and nonchalantly strolled toward Dane.

" 'Oh, I am a gay caballero,' " he hummed softly, " 'An' exceedingly gay caballero —' "

"Never mind that," Dane growled at him. "You may not feel so gay time I get done with you. Know anything about bullet wounds?"

"A leetle," the Mexican admitted cautiously.

"We'll see. Lead off up this crack, an' remember — one false move's all I'm askin'."

They came, presently, into the little pocket where Dane had left the unconscious Jupe. Dolton was still there, body propped on an elbow, open eyes glaring round him, face twisted with pain and balked anger.

"Ha!" he snarled. "Decided to come after all, eh?" He threw his head back, laughed at them wildly. The laugh choked off in a hoarse kind of croak and Jupe came lurching upright, twin spots of color burning in his cheeks, the light of some mad purpose balefully staring from his eyes. His gaze was not fixed on either of them, but between them and beyond them. With an amazing speed he jerked his pistol. "Stand where you are, Jack Ketchum! By God I got you dead to rights!"

He took a half-step forward, staggered and collapsed.

Kin Savvy jerked a surreptitious look behind him; crossed himself when he found nobody there.

"He's out of his head," Dane said. "Take a look at him." And he kicked Jupe's fallen weapon out of Kin Savvy's reach. The way Jupe lay now he showed one side of his shirt dark and stiff with clotted blood. His pain-pinched cheeks were white and drawn, and it seemed like he could not last the hour out.

Kin Savvy, clucking to himself like some old hen, knelt down by Jupe's side; got his shirt open, carefully cut it off with a long-bladed knife from his boot top and explored Jupe's side with the tender touch of a woman.

Dane could see how the blood was oozing from that puckered blue-black hole and wished he had Bufe's knowledge — Bufe's experience of these things. He dreaded the thought of Dulcey's look when he told her — as he surely must — that her brother Jupe was dead.

Kin Savvy said, laying Jupe back on the ground, "Ees not bad hurt. Only got one wound — old one — bus' open; she's lose one pile of blood. Be all right two-t'ree days. Bes' stay here — take eet easy. Too moch riding no good for them wound."

He commenced tearing Jupe's shirt into strips. "Canteen on my saddle."

Scooping up Jupe's gun Dane fetched

152

the canteen. He helped Kin Savvy cleanse the wound, watched while the Mexican deftly bound it. Lucky, Dane thought, it was cool in here; the wind sucked in from the gulch did that, and there were junipers on the cliff above that would keep the sunlight out. It made an ideal place for Jupe to rest up — provided Stroat's men didn't search the pass by daylight. He could rub out their tracks but he couldn't well hide the fissure.

He looked up, found the Mexican eying him. "You got a fifty-fifty chance of gettin' out of this alive," he said. "Start talkin'."

He lifted Jupe's six-shooter from the waistband of his Levis, suggestively twirling it by the trigger guard. "I want the whole truth, hombre, an' the first piece of a lie I catch you in is goin' to be your last."

Kin Savvy grinned.

"I ain't foolin'," Dane said. "Start talkin'."

"I 'ave show you them paper —"

"Never mind the paper!"

Kin Savvy shrugged. "What you wan' know?"

"I wanta know why you led us into that trap last night! What kind of game are you playin'?"

"*Caramba!* She's no game I'm play!

Thees paper, she's on level," Kin Savvy said, hauling it out of his shirt. "Thees paper say I'm Rurale — say I'm up here for catch stole horses. Ees truth! I'm go for get the job with Ketchum but them Black Jack, she's catch on to me — try for keel me — twice! *Mira* — look! I tell you!"

The Señorita Yolanda Dolores García y Trujillo, daughter of an ancient Spanish family and owner of Rancho Grande in Sonora, had recently lost a herd of valuable blooded mares — palominos, descended from the famous horses of Maximilian. She had reported the theft to the Rurales who, on checking back, had found the circumstances at once both bizarre and suspicious. A strange rider had been seen in the vicinity of the señorita's ranch, an unknown Yankee, who had spent a deal of time at a local cantina of ill repute. The man had come into the country on a pinto cow horse with a fine Morgan stallion in tow. He was anxious, he said to sell the horse, and had papers to show it belonged to him. But he had turned down at least four handsome offers. He had gone finally to the Rancho Grande and had interested its owner in his stallion; she had offered him seven hundred and fifty pesos, but the man had laughed at this offer, claiming the stallion was worth twice as much. He had lingered on for a while at the cantina, then one dark night had departed; and it was found upon the following morning that the Señorita Yolanda's herd of palomino mares had also gone. "Them stallion," Kin Savvy declared, "was use' to lure them away."

The Rurales had sifted facts and done considerable trailing. It was ascertained that the gringo had headed north. They found where he had crossed the border, but there had been no sign of the palominos or of his stallion. Kin Savvy had finally cut their sign twenty miles north of Rancho Grande; they had been heading north by east. By the sign no rider had been with them. The mares had been following the stallion.

"A clever treeck," Kin Savvy said; "but me, I'm seen thees gringo before w'en she 'ave live in Texas. I'm go there, make some talk aroun' —"

"What's all that got to do with —"

"But I'm *tell* you — thees Gringo go by Black Jack Ketchum."

"Mean to say it was Ketchum grabbed those horses?"

"*Seguro,* Miguel! Eet was them Black Jack! Sleek hombre, eh?"

"You'll play hell tryin' to prove it!" Dane

155

said, half forgetting his anger and suspicion in his interest for the tale. "This Ketchum's nobody's fool —"

"Ees truth — *verdad!*" Kin Savvy nodded, shaking his head emphatically. "Rurales not want Ketchum; I'm come for get them caballos. Look: eet say so in thees paper."

He thrust the thing at Telldane; and Dane, one eye cocked watchfully, read it through from end to end. It was as the man had claimed. He'd been sent up after the horses and the paper asked for the cooperation of the American authorities in running the palominos down. He had the necessary papers to prove Rancho Grande ownership; and the García y Trujillo picture brand was stamped on each animal's off hip.

Dane handed the papers back, regarded Kin Savvy dubiously. "That still don't explain how come you run us into that trap or —"

"But I 'ave not feenish'," Kin Savvy protested. "Leesten!"

He had followed the horses, not the man. The trail had led him through this Llano Estacado, across the greasewood flats and up into the Sierra Negras. There it had vanished completely. For two weeks he had drifted through the hills in futile search, finally to come upon Ketchum's ranch and, recognizing the man, to get a job there.

Getting the job had been easy, Kin Savvy said — "like fall off log." But all the time Ketchum's men had watched him like a gang of hawks. Any investigations carried on had to be managed with utmost stealth; and, even so, they'd finally caught him prowling one day in the brakes off west of the ranch. They'd asked no questions, said not a word, but from that day on he'd been given chores that kept him round head-quarters; and no matter what the time of night there was always somebody watching him.

Then one night he could stand it no longer. He was getting no place and the constant surveillance was getting on his nerves. He asked Ketchum for his time; said he guessed he'd try Arizona — too cold, this country, for him. "You'll find hell a damn' sight warmer," Ketchum declared, getting out of his chair; and with a hard grin reached for his pistol.

Kin Savvy knew what was coming. He didn't hesitate a second, but dragging his gun, sprang sideways, flinging himself through the ranch-house window. A saddled horse was by the porch and Kin Savvy took it, his departure sped by a hail of bullets. Town had seemed the safest place and he'd headed for it pronto, aiming to seek out Sheriff Stroat.

"I'm saw heem," he said, grinning wryly. "He say I'm crazy in the head. Jack Ketchum honest man — me, I'm dream all thees. I guess so! Me, I'm go corral for get my horse. Them Black Jack come, try for gon me. Then you come — we turn table."

Dane took a deep breath and shook off the spell of the Mexican's talking. "That's all very well," he grunted. "Mebbe that's so an' mebbe it ain't — but it don't explain last night by a jugful! If you're such a fine, upstandin' cuss —"

"*Pues, mira* — look!" Kin Savvy said. "I 'ave not feenish! Them Señor Shereef, she's tell me other day eef I'm help get thees hombre, Jupe Dolton, w'y then w'en we 'ave got heem, the Shereef she weel mebbeso look into thees beezness of my horses. So —" Kin Savvy spread his graceful hands in a shrug of Latin eloquence. "Las' night when that Jackman come an' say Shereef on way weeth posse, I'm theenk like hell. I'm get the — w'at you call — *perspiration*. I'm say to myself, 'Jesus María, it ees time you got them caballos!' W'en Shereef come I pass heem high sign

— bleenk the eye. W'en you're not look he shape the lips, say, 'Pleano Pass' an' I'm nod to heem."

"Just a white chip in a no-limit game, eh?" Telldane said sarcastically. But it was clear enough now how the sheriff had been able to track them down so fast, so unerringly, last night. He eyed Kin Savvy pityingly. "An' you think Stroat'll keep his part of the bargain?"

The big Mex chuckled, languid shoulders rising and squaring, lines of amusement shaping his mouth. "I'm not bank too moch on eet. But w'en the devil she's drive —"

"Never mind the old saws. I know 'em all by heart," Dane said. "The main point is, you led us into a trap — deliberately. Knowing Jupe Dolton might well be killed without one chance for his alley; that his sister —"

"How could I guess the señorita would be weeth us? As for Jupe Dolton, he's outlaw any'ow — use' to bullets. W'at's extra handful more or less to hombre like heem? Besides —"

"Yeah! Besides everything else, the trap you rode us into was cocked with Ketchum rifles. *Ketchum!* Your sworn enemy — the man who is hunting your scalp and who —

according to your tell — ran off with the Rancho Grande remuda!"

"*Válgame Dios!* It was a treeck!" Kin Savvy cried, and the light of his snapping eyes showed suddenly bleak as gun steel. "You theenk I'm know them Black Jack, she's be there? *Caramba — no!* Them damn Stroat, she's treeck me — she's try for get my goddam face shot off! Kin Savvy, she's no fool! Can look through piece of glass so fast as anyone! Thees Shereef, she's crooked lak dog hind leg!"

Dane eyed him searchingly. "Not crooked," he said, "— just sore. Mad enough to chaw the sights off a six-gun; an' you can't wholly blame him. After all, he's got a rep at stake —"

"Rep!" Kin Savvy snorted; snapped his fingers contemptuously. "I got a rep myself, me! You got rep! Jupe Dolton, she's got rep, by Chris'! I guess we got good right for chaw the seexgon too!"

A faint grin twisted Dane's lips. "I guess we have at that," he said, and let the matter drop. "How'd you happen to be ridin' through the Pass this mornin'?"

"I'm search for you; I'm weesh for tell you 'bout las' *noches.* I'm got for get them caballos — theenk mebbeso you an' Jupe she's help me. No?"

"You willin' to help us round up Ketchum?" Dane asked after a moment's consideration; and Kin Savvy nodded violently.

"Nothing I like better! You got rope? By Chris', I like for dab it on heem!"

12

Dry-Gulched

Dane, leaving Kin Savvy to guard the pocket and take care of Jupe, shortly after sunup rode off on the Mexican's stolen horse to hunt for Dolton's sister. There was anger in him, a gathered anger sprung from last night's need for turning this girl adrift. He was concerned for her, more worried than he cared to admit, because she'd come to mean a lot to him — all any woman ever *could* mean. For Dane Telldane she spelled perfection, completeness — all that a sorry world could ever hold for him. But the anger in him went far deeper than concern for the girl could have thrust it; it was cumulative, built up of divers small things. The blind pigheadedness of Sheriff Stroat, the flagrant injustices with which this raw land abounded, the schemes and trickery and killings — all these had their place in it, composing a dark and vicious pattern that was like a rasp to his nerves.

At the Siding events moved on apace, and the pace was not a smooth one. Big

Rail Frisby, the Rock Island super, stepped into Rolsem's bar and across it, briefly nodding to an early-morning lounger who was watching the swamper work. "Sheriff back there?" Frisby asked of the half-awake barman, and jerked a nod at the door to the private room. The barman, wiping sweat from his bleary eyes, said "I guess so," and Frisby stepped through the door; closed it carefully.

Alex Stroat, half asleep with his head on his arms, jerked erect at the sound; loosed a curse when he saw the visitor's identity. "A great adviser *you* are! Solomon Frisby! *Christ!*"

"My advice is a damned sight better," Frisby murmured, "than your ability as a sheriff." He stared at the lawman uncharitably. "Pull yourself together — you look like the wrath of God. Want a drink?"

The sheriff made a grimace; looked at himself in the gilt-framed mirror that was hung above the sideboard. Scowling he wet his fingers, passing them through his tousled hair. He loosened the faded scarf about his throat and cuffed some of the dust from his clothing. "I been a goddam fool!" he blurted.

Rail Frisby eyed him consideringly, slowly nodded.

Stroat glared at him. "I've played hell!"

"Never mind," Frisby said. "We all do some time or other. What particular hell have you played — besides lettin' Dolton slip through your hands again?"

The sheriff dropped back in his chair with a groan, put his fists on the table and stared at them. "I've over-reached myself — by grab, they'll have my badge for this . . . I've gone beyond my jurisdiction —"

"You mean the Pass? It wasn't exactly brilliant — the story's all over town. But you were inside your jurisdiction; Quay County cuts further south than that. The Llano's well inside the border. An' as for deputizin' Ketchum's men —"

The sheriff shoved all that aside. "That!" he said, and snorted. He pounded a fist on the table bitterly. "It's the girl I'm talkin' about! The town ain't found —"

"What girl?" Frisby's glance at Stroat was startled.

"Dolton's sister — I've grabbed her!" Stroat growled.

The Rock Island super whistled. He said: "Swell! I never thought you'd have the wit! Why —"

But Stroat wasn't listening. He said worriedly: "An' I turned her horse loose with a note for Jupe on the — What the hell you grinnin' at?" he snarled, breaking off and glaring. "What's so goddam funny?"

"That wasn't laughter. What you seen was a chuckle of triumph — of pure appreciation," Frisby declared, and slapped his leg at the prospect. "This town," he said, getting out his pipe and filling it, "has been underestimating you. Stroat, I take my hat off; you couldn't have handled it better —"

"Better?" Stroat eyed him suspiciously. "What's that supposed to mean?"

"Just what I said — better!" Frisby lit his pipe, took a few puffs, sat down and hitched his chair up to face Stroat across the table. He took a few more puffs consideringly while he mulled the thought in his mind. "I believe we've got 'em licked — by God, I believe you've solved it!"

"What the hell are you talkin' about? Put it in English, can't you?"

"Look here," Frisby said, tapping the table with his pipe bowl. "We've been tryin' for weeks to lay Jupe Dolton by the heels an' put an end to this blasted train robbin'. But up to now he's got away every time — just like he did last night. But all that's past an' done with; we got him where we want him now — thanks to this bright thought of yours. You couldn't have done a better stroke of business than grabbing that girl —"

"I'm glad you think so," Stroat said resentfully; "but from where I sit the prospects look anything but cheerful. They'll prob'ly have my star for this. Why —" He appeared aghast at his own temerity. "Why, damn it, Rail! I had no right to —"

"Tut, tut," Frisby grinned; "an' again tut. No one's goin' to open his mouth. In a case like this you got a right to do most anything you think of if it's like to get Jupe Dolton caught. The man's a murderer!"

"His sister ain't." The sheriff passed a hand across his cheeks and groaned. "We ain't got a thing against her —"

Frisby snorted. "The hell we ain't! Been harborin' a known fugitive, ain't she? What if he *is* her brother? He's a killin', murderin' thief an' — Where you got this girl at, anyway?"

The star packer told him and Frisby chuckled. "All right," he said. "All we got to do is keep our eyes on the place an' sooner or later Dolton will show. An' when he does, we grab him!"

It was approaching dusk when Dane rode into the Pass again. He'd been in the saddle pretty nearly all day, and he'd had no sleep the night before, and he was weary to the bone — dog-weary. All the bars of his vigilance were down. He rode with his chin digging into his chest, rifle scabbarded, eyes half closed, dozing by fits and starts — unable, despite cognizance of his danger, to keep his wits about him. All the reserves of his strength were spent and he rode like a man with his guts shot out, forward keeled across the saddle.

He was that way when a rifle slammed its echoes against the gulch — rather, he was that way when it spoke. When its echoes struck the sandstone walls he was toppling from the saddle. He hit sprawled out like a busted sack; stayed where he dropped, limp, motionless.

13

"Git Back!"

High above the Pass, feathers sharply defined by the dying sun, a buzzard sailed on outspread wings, wheeling in graceful circles, each loop lower than the one before. It seemed but another moment must see it drop in swift descent to the facedown figure sprawled moveless on the darkening trail. Indeed, its drop was started when with a raucous squawk it broke from its slant and fled away on flapping wings.

From a rocky shoulder of the gulch's left wall a man's hatted head and shoulders rose into the last red rays of the dying sun; rose slowly, cautiously, yet withal triumphantly. He stepped from his covert, rifle ready. Erect he stood and warily watched the man in the trail for some further moments before, leading his horse, he started down toward the man he had dropped with drygulch lead.

And then it happened.

Telldane's right shoulder abruptly twitched. In the dusk something flashed and flame streaked the murk. The man with the rifle staggered and screamed. The rifle fell out of his hands and he stumbled backward with arms out-flailing, a tragic gesture. It was the last he made. His body struck the rocks of the floor and went still — still and crumpled.

Dane got to his feet. Grimly he slapped the dust from his clothes. Blew the smoke from his pistol and thrust it away. Then he straightened, strode over to where the man lay. It was Trotter — Morgan Trotter. Jack Ketchum's man Friday.

He was dead.

Leading Trotter's horse Telldane rode into the Pass. All the sleep jarred out of him he rode stiffly erect, a somber shape in the thickening dusk. But for the haste of Trotter's triggering finger he would now be where Morgan Trotter was, fit bait for that buzzard. A man's life caught up with him. It was a lesson and a warning. Only Trotter's haste and a habit built up of three years of this danger had saved Dane Telldane; and he broodingly knew it. This was how his brother, Bufe, would some time go. It was the way of their kind. It made a man think.

Telldane was still thinking when he tied

the two horses at the base of the fissure. Voices reached him, wrangling, downswung through the quiet on the breeze being steadily sucked from the cranny. Jupe had wakened apparently and, as usual, was querulous. Like enough he was wanting to kill Kin Savvy. Another like Bufe, this Jupe Dolton, Dane thought; and unless he mended his ways he would go like Bufe — like brash Morgan Trotter. Like some others Dane knew.

Filled with this mood Dane strode into the pocket. Kin Savvy was holding Jupe back with a leveled six gun. Jupe was wild-eyed and cursing, face twisted with hatred. Kin Savvy was saying: ". . . no diff'rence! Me, I'm no put the trust een you. Geef you the gon an' off you go — *ees verdad!* — like the w'irrelwind! Ah! *Válgame Dios* — you are back!" he cried relievedly, glance flashing sideways toward Dane with real pleasure. "Mebbeso you can put the sense in these hombre's cabeza!"

"How is he?"

"I'm all right; there's nothin' wrong with *me!*" Jupe snapped. "But *you* — I'm here to say you oughta hev yore head examined! Of all the damn-fool — Mean to say you're *trustin'* that — that sneakin', double-dealin' coyote of a — *Hell!*" Descriptive words of sufficient potency appeared to fail Jupe. He glared wildly, shouted: "Gimme a gun! Goddam you! Gimme a gun an' let —"

"*Shut up!*" Dane, striding forward, slapped Jupe twice across the face. Rocking, open-handed blows that stopped Jupe's profane, blustering threats in mid-flow and left him gaping, gasping — inarticulate; like a fish yanked out of water.

"Now sit down on that rock an' listen!" Dane growled, and in words of one-syllable proceeded to explain the Mexican's place in this thing. When he quit Jupe sat there sullen and silent, a too-bright flush on his pale, pinched cheeks and his thin mouth twisted in a plain disbelief.

"Well?"

"You can swaller that hogwash if you want," he said thickly, "— if you're that big a fool. But *me* — Takes more'n a passel of slick chin music to pull the wool over *my* eyes! This greaser's just what I said las' night — a spyin', back-stabbin' polecat; an' if you're goin' to turn him loose like an ol' bell mare you might's well hand me over to Stroat right now an' be done with it!"

Dane eyed him bleakly. Kin Savvy shrugged. Shoving pistol in leather he was wheeling away when Dane said sharply: "Where *you* off to?"

Kin Savvy's smile was unpleasant. "You theenk I'm stay here aftair leesten to all them name? By Chris', I got some pride, me! Thees hombre, she can go for hell! Bah!" he spat, looking across his nose at Jupe contemptuously. "We got word for heem, back dere in Sonora —" He pulled himself up, ramrod-straight; and his eyes flashed arrogance great as Jupe's own. "I am Bobadilla — Jesús María Bobadilla! My people, she is come from Castile, by Chris', an' me I'm don' have for take such talk from any damn' greengo peeg!"

"By grab!" Dane glared. "You goin' to act up, too?" Exasperation nearly got the best of him. Then the humor of the situation struck through his weariness, through his anger; and he got a grip on his lifting temper. He had need of this man; he must talk him out of leaving them.

But it took a deal of tact and persuasion to soothe the Mexican's ruffled feathers. The sting of Jupe's epithets rankled, and the gratuitous slurs with which Dolton punctuated Dane's remarks served to keep Kin Savvy's temper up.

At last Dane with an angry snort was about to quit the place himself when hoof sound, echoing up the gorge, froze him stiff in his tracks, tensely crouched, head canted. His eyes met Kin Savvy's — locked in grim knowledge. Premonition leaped from the Mexican's stare, and a dropped hand tugged the gun from his belt. "By gar!" he breathed softly, and darted forward with Dane, cat-footed, following hard on his heels.

No rider showed in the murk of the Pass; but a horse was there, head dropped to the trail, not a stone's throw away from the two Dane had tied there. And Kin Savvy, grabbing hold of Dane, pointed to a vague patch of paleness against the dark saddle. "Wait!" he grunted while Dane was still staring; and slipped quietly away through the wind-riffled shadows.

He was back almost at once with the horse in tow; and Dane swore. Swore under his breath while a cold fear clutched him. For the horse was his own — the one he'd ridden last night. The one Dulcey'd been riding when he sent her away!

The white thing was paper, tied fast to the saddle. With shaking fingers Dane ripped it loose. The big Mex cupped a match in his palms while Dane, bent forward, read it.

"What's it say? Goddam you, tell me what's that writin'!"

Dane straightened, thrust Jupe off his

173

shoulder roughly. The match went out in Kin Savvy's hand and they stood in darkness with the rasp of Jupe's breathing. Kin Savvy said: "Señor! What ees it?"

The moments dragged before Dane spoke. He said in tones that were choked with anger: "They've got her! Stroat has grabbed Dulcey!"

The Mexican gasped. Jupe Dolton said nothing; and when Dane awoke to the implication he found Jupe crouched with a foot in the stirrup, wild-eyed, pistol leveled — a pistol he'd snatched from Telldane's own holster.

"Get back!" Jupe snarled. "Don't try to stop me! *I'll* get her loose, by God! *Git back in that cranny!*"

"Jupe —"

But Jupe was gone.

14

Dark Hunger

Dane and Kin Savvy stared at each other. The sound of Jupe's flight fell away in the distance. Then suddenly, furiously, Telldane cursed; and the big Mex nodded with a rare understanding.

"W'at horse he ride?"

"Trotter's," Dane said, and explained how it got there. "I don't know how many miles the bronc's good for — prob'ly plenty. Trotter acted like he'd been forted up all day just waitin' for one of us to show; which means Jack Ketchum's been usin' his head. What I started to say though is no matter how far Trotter's bronc can go, Jupe'll never hang on clear to the Siding — he *can't!* No man could in his condition. He's clean out of his head or he'd not be tryin'. Stroat won't hurt Dulcey — it's a trick to bring Jupe in — wonder they didn't think of it sooner. I can see the slick hand of Rail Frisby —"

"Me, I can see a rope-tie —"

"A what?"

Kin Savvy twirled a quick hand round his head; gave brief pantomime of cowhands hauling on a rope. "Like that," he said with a grimace. "We got for head heem off —"

"Sure — but *how?*" Dane growled disgustedly. "Jupe could find these trails with his eyes shut — we don't know 'em at all; leastways we don't know the cut-offs Jupe'll be ridin'."

Dane slammed both hands deep into his pockets, took a savage turn in the hoof-tracked sand. "Damn it, it's too late now to keep him from Stroat —"

"We got the good caballos — fly like wind. Thees horse she's belong for Black Jack — Jeez Chris'! We two good horse thief, no? Ought to get job hees gang!"

"Hold on —" Dane grunted, and stood there tensely. "That's an idea, fella —"

"Can talk tomorrow. Now good time for ride. Better we ride queeck," Kin Savvy hinted, "or thees Jupe, she's get the ride on rope!"

"You're right," Dane snapped, and reached for the pommel of the saddled bronc which had brought the note. They piled in the hulls and swung their leathers; Dane gripping his reins with a heavy pressure, his jaws hard clamped and his eyes gone slitted. This might be pay-off. It was sure to be hell any way you took it.

They rushed through the ink-black night like bullets, forward-bent in their saddles, nagged and whipsawed by the need for speed.

An empty land, this through which they rode. Cow country — a region of scattered ranches where men called themselves neighbors who lived forty miles apart. To the left rose the dark, bleak bulk of Mesa Redonda; but ahead the night was an unrelieved black from which things jumped, fled past and were gone in the murk behind.

Dane's thinking caught up with him and he said abruptly, gruffly: "You fellas put anything in your bellies? I'm tryin' to figure how long Jupe can stand it!" He had to shout to make himself heard above the flog of their hoofbeats.

But the Mexican nodded. "I foun' antelope in saddle bags — some fool was goin' for take thees caballo on treep. I make leedle fire . . . Agua in tinaja — make leedle soup. Jupe eat heem. Say taste like wash my sock — ask eef I cook my saddle?"

Jupe might make town, Dane conceded reluctantly. He might if he had not lost too much blood. But he was tough, like most of the denizens of this country — a hard land that bred hard men; and Jupe was inured to hardship from those months he'd hid out from Stroat's cursing posses. Yes! The fool would most likely make it and get himself grabbed by Stroat's planted gunslicks.

He thought of Ketchum — of last night's battle. Black Jack was playing a deep, deep game. He had the cards gripped close to his chest and Dane couldn't read them — couldn't even guess them. No mere desire to apprehend fugitives had placed Jack Ketchum in that gulch last night; he'd been there of grim purpose, there to see Jupe planted — and he hadn't cared much who got planted with him so long as he got Dolton's light blown out. A mighty queer thing, the way Dane viewed it. Ketchum stood to lose a heap more by Jupe's death than he'd ever gain. For as long as Jupe lived he was Ketchum's best alibi. Why was Jack Ketchum so anxious to kill him?

And Max Jackman's son, Luce: Where did *he* fit this picture? What had made him so certain he'd find Jupe at the ranch? Had this big Mex, Kin Savvy, really called the turn when he said Luce must have been watching the place from some hide-out with glasses? And if so, *why?* What had Jackman to gain from a play like that?

Dane shook his head, grumbled, sore baffled. Luce Jackman, if he *had* been watching the place, might have been doing so on Dulcey's account; keeping an eye on the place to make sure she was not molested by any of the gun-slick drifters who of late had been roaming the country like lobos, alert for any loot that offered.

Who had burned Jupe's initials onto that knife hilt, then driven the blade into Jack Ketchum's woman? For Sprawly Clark, Kin Savvy had claimed . . .

Dane shook his head; swore bitterly. A crazy, mixed-up mess of cross-purposes — like a nightmare, it was, the way things were happening. But one thing he saw with a vivid clarity — Jupe's innocence. Jupe might be a cow thief but he was no train robber; he hadn't the brains for a coup of that size, nor the firmness or temper to carry the thing off. The man who was grabbing the Rock Island pay rolls week after week was a cool, cool hand — no brash, rattlebrained hothead like Jupe. And there was too much evidence against him for Jupe to be the murderer of Sprawly Clark; that knife, the hat and the gilded heel. And finally, to clinch the case above all else, she had been Ketchum's woman, and Jupe had been seeing her.

One other thing struck Dane like a hammer — it was useless to make any plans in this country. Events moved too fast for a man's calculation. There could be no planning, for nothing stood still. This was a land bred for trouble, blood-letting, black turbulence. A place where none but the gunfighter breed could survive.

The night paled in the east to the rising moon, and far across the greasewood flats the northernmost bluffs of the Llano were lifting their serrated outline like a backdrop chopped from cardboard.

If —

He never finished the thought.

Out yonder was tumult — a swift blur of movement. Wind rushed wild sound from an oncoming pony. A clatter of slithering hoofs cleaved the ghost-gloom before them and a rider's shape loomed against the sky. An oath broke from Kin Savvy as he sawed on his reins. Dane, jerking his pistol, cried harshly: "*Hold it!* Sing out by God, or I'll let you have it!"

A gasp. A quick cry. Then Dulcey's voice — tumbled words thick with feeling. "Dane! Dane — is it really *you?*"

"Jupe!" Dane shouted. *"Dulcey!* Where is he?"

"They've got him — Stroat's grabbed him! They've got him at Rolsem's!"

15

"I'll Take My Chance on That!"

Somewhat earlier in the evening — about the time Dane Telldane had been dropping Morgan Trotter — a portentous conference was being held in the room behind Rolsem's bar. Grimly seated round the rough pine table that served Hake both as desk and as eating place were Max Jackman, repping for the cattle crowd and given odds of ten to one on being next choice for Territorial Governor; Rail Frisby, taking care of the Rock Island's interests; Alex Stroat, championing law and order; and the mountainous Hake himself. Those four — comptrollers of the country's destiny.

Max Jackman spoke for the cattle because he had the inalienable right to do so — the right of power and influence. But he'd been more than merely a nursemaid to a bunch of long-horned cattle; in his time he'd been a miner, banker, stockman. He had built up with the country. A charitable man, and merciless; he was hearty, florid, bland — a power. He was many things to many men, but spokesman for them all. He said: "I want to know, Stroat, what you've done about this business."

Sheriff Stroat squirmed round in his chair and fingered the grip of his collar. He put his big soft hands on the table and drummed at it with his fingers. He ran a tongue across his lips, began to clear his throat when Jackman interrupted gruffly — a cold-eyed man with florid cheeks and heavy brows, with heavy mustache and a cigar as black usually protruding from a corner of the tight-lipped mouth beneath it. He said sharply: "What *have* you done?"

"I've done all a man could do," Stroat growled. "If —"

"Have you put Jupe Dolton back of bars?"

A high roan color flagged the sheriff's apoplectic cheeks, and his eyes took fire from the blaze of anger riding him. With a snarl he came half out of his chair. "You know damn well I haven't!" He banged the table with his fist, ignoring the way the glasses jumped; banged it again, defiantly. "What the hell do you think I am — *the Army of the West?*" He glared at Jackman bitterly. "If I had the men —"

"Why haven't you had them? Your bills

183

for service are big enough. How many men do you need?"

Stroat's tobacco-stained teeth clamped down on his lip, biting back the heady anger that was roweling his cheeks. "I'll need a damned sight more'n I've had so far if you expect me to get results," he snarled. "That goddam Dolton's a will-o'the-wisp! I've laid trap after trap —"

"Perhaps," Jackman said, eyes glittering a little, "what we need's a new broom for this job."

"Then by God," said Stroat through bared teeth, "you'd better get it!" Flouncing out of his chair, he ripped the badge from his shirt and slammed it on the table, and wheeled like a wet cat toward the door.

Frisby caught at his arm. "Hold on!" he said; and to Jackman: "Stroat's doin' all any man could do, Max. There's no use raggin' him about it. There ain't a man in this country could do more —"

"My son could," Jackman said coolly.

Frisby threw out his hands, and Rolsem, leaning forward, said: "But hell's fire, Max, you don't want Luce mixed up in this!"

"I want this train robbing stopped," Jackman said. "This is *my* country — *I'm* the one that gets talked about whenever this train-robbing's mentioned! That part

184

was bad enough; but now they're callin' this country a killers' paradise! This business has put the country back twenty years — the flow of immigration's dwindlin' — it's swinging clear around us. An' it'll keep on swinging around us long as that pack of gun-waving hoodlums Jupe Dolton's collected are allowed to run loose and terrorize —"

"What do you suggest?" Frisby said.

Jackman grimaced. "I've already suggested that the U.S. marshal's office send somebody down to investigate; but if anyone's been sent down they've certainly not talked with *me*." He looked at Stroat. "Any deputy marshals dropped in to visit with you?"

"No." The sheriff said it sourly, and turned again to depart.

But once more Frisby stopped him. "Keep your shirt on, Alex. Max knows you're a good man — he's just got a little excited. Probably been losin' a lot of cows to that bunch —"

Maxwell Jackman snorted. "I can stand the goddam rustlin'! They been gettin' plenty, but I can stand that — it's the effect this hell-raising has on the country's growth that's rilin' my dander up! Why —"

"Well, I think I can safely say," Frisby

cut in, "that these ructions have about reached the end of their rope — Jupe Dolton has, anyway." He winked at the sheriff mysteriously.

"What's that?" Jackman said, leaning forward.

Frisby chuckled. "Alex an' me, we been figurin'," he said. "Jupe's a hotheaded young fool — we've known that all along, of course. But now we've taken it into account. We've got a trap baited this time I don't believe he'll skin through. We've got his sister —"

He broke off, startled by the look of Jackman's eyes.

"You've *what?*"

The tone of those words was ominous. Alex Stroat started sweating and Hake Rolsem seemed to have a hard time breathing. But Frisby said coolly: "We're holding Jupe's sister as a material witness —"

"You fools!" Jackman rasped; and his cold eyes glittered balefully as they raked the sheriff's face. "By God, they'll have your star for this!"

Into the choked, dread silence Frisby drawled, "I don't think so, Max — can't agree with you at all. They ought to vote Sheriff Stroat a medal. I offer it as my opinion that Jupe Dolton, so soon as he learns that we are holding his sister here, will come hellbending to her rescue. In which case, the sheriff and his deputies will arrest him. Without his leadership the gang will break up and these robberies and other acts of outlawry will automatically cease."

For dragging seconds Maxwell Jackman sat motionless with his cold eyes searching the Rock Island super's face. "You said 'here,' I think. Are you holding the girl in *this* place? Here in this —"

There were shouts out front, a sudden commotion. A rider's boots broke echoes from the barroom floor. The thin door shook to a heavy fist and a man's voice shouted: "You in there, Alex? *Alex!*" The voice was high-pitched, strained with excited elation. "We've got him — *we've got Jupe Dalton!*"

Dane Telldane sat statue-still with both fists locked to the saddle horn. His lips moved soundlessly and stopped, the muscles of his lean hard jaw standing out like a steer-strained rope. His look, with the moon's silver bright upon his face, held them tense and silent — abashed. It was like a face chopped out of granite, implacable, relentless. "I'll meet you at the corral. Take Dulcey and break out fresh broncs for the four of us. Don't be seen if you can help it, but if that windy wrangler spots you, tie him up an' gag him. If anyone else chips into the ante throw your gun on 'em pronto!"

"Dane!" Dulcey cried. "Where are you going?"

"I'm goin' to get Jupe Dolton out of there!"

"Dane? You *can't!*" Dulcey's voice was thin with fright. "You'll never make it! They'll —"

"I'll take my chance on that —"

"Dane — Dane!" she cried, beside herself, throwing her horse in front of him. "Dane, are you crazy? You can't — Why, Stroat's got men all over town! They're hid out, watching for you! Stroat's told them to shoot on sight — I *heard* him!"

She caught his arm, anxious face uptilted, pleading glance hard-searching his cheeks. "Tell me you won't do this crazy thing — Oh, *Dane!* Can't you *see?* It's all so useless — don't do it, Dane!"

Telldane moistened his lips. But he could find no words to say to her.

She said impetuously: "Jupe's guilty, Dane — he's been stealing cattle — running off whenever he could. It's a wild streak in him —"

"He never killed Sprawly Clark!" Dane gritted. "An' he never stopped those trains —"

"But don't you *see?* Even if you get him loose it will just be the same thing over again; they'll keep hunting and hunting, and in the end they'll get him. Listen! He's my brother, Dane, and it's hard, *bitter* hard, to see it; but Jupe's not worth this risk. Dane! Promise me! Promise . . ."

Dulcey's voice trailed off.

In the gash of moonlight Dane sat moveless, sat still with that fixed, granite look on his face.

With a dry, choking sob of despair Dulcey turned, turned away from him, blindly driving her horse at the night.

Dane's fumbling fingers built a smoke — twitched it savagely away from him, a fluttering thing of shreds and paper. His stare raked the Mexican's cheeks; and he picked up his reins.

"Take care of her, boy," he said; and was gone at a wild crashing gallop, his bronc's flaring nostrils pointed straight for the town.

16

The Dark Gods Laugh

And that was the way he entered it — wild riding, larruping in at a headlong gallop, a gun in each fist and a yell on his lips, ripping up the echoes and tearing the crouched stillness of the place to shreds. Experience shaped this strategy; all the tales Bufe had ever told him bolstered it. *Feed 'em the fear of God!*

Every hired gun, every drifting bravo in town, would be on the lookout for him, gunfighter-fashion — it was the way of their kind. Dane understood it. He was of that breed himself. All up and down the block-long street lights winked out and windows rattled as he thundered by with six guns flaming. Then he whirled and circled — dashed back again with a jumping rifle across his hip. He dodged the corral, came up back of the shanties on the opposite side from Rolsem's bar. Toward the tracks he pounded with the piled cans scattering 'neath the gelding's hoofs while he thumbed fresh loads to his heated pistols and the night went wild with their shouts and curses, with the *crack-crack-crack* of their frenzied salvos. They might as well have fired at the moon! He laughed at them, taunted them, called them damned feisty dogs; and they roared from their shelters with the snarl of a wolf pack, rushed for the tracks like rattleheaded fools.

Which was what he'd been angling for.

A bleak grin tugged his lips as he sheathed smoking pistols and ground-tied his horse out back of the land office where the fernlike fronds of a pepper tree added measurably to the gloom.

They had lost him just as he'd hoped they would. He could hear them noisily milling round among the sidings where the boxcar homes of the section hands reared oblongs of light and shadow. Dane turned away, content to leave them to the tempers of Rail Frisby's micks.

Dane trotted on, curled into the gloom back of Rolsem's bar. He paused there a second, slid along the adobe wall till he could see the hitchrack with its huddle of nervous, fretting horses; then he cat-footed back. The tumult was growing off there by the sidings. Dane put his shoulder to the door and pushed inside with a gun in his right fist, cocked and lifted.

Jupe was there, in a chair, with his head on the table, the others grouped round him: Stroat and a deputy, Rolsem, Rail Frisby and a long-geared gent with cold eyes and a black-mustached mouth clamped round a cigar — Max Jackman, Dane guessed. Alex Stroat was talking; and Dane's lips thinned, briefly touched by a smile as he stood, undiscovered, a moment taking in the scene.

"No use you countin' on Telldane," Stroat was growling at Jupe.

But Dolton was in no shape to listen. If he wasn't clean out, he was mighty near it; and Dane's mouth tightened, for he'd been counting on Jupe's help.

There was nothing new in this picture for the brother of Bufe Telldane. It followed an old, familiar pattern with the bracket lamps' light showing up the grim faces that were set and waiting for the prisoner to speak.

Jupe finally, bleary-eyed, rose to an elbow and cursed them thickly. " 'F you know all the answers, then what're y'u rantin' for? Go on, y'u bastards! String me up an' —" He broke off, wide-sprung eyes fixed startled on Dane. And something Stroat read in the quick, desperate hope of that stare swung him round, right hand reaching.

"Evening, folks. Sheriff Stroat, I believe," Telldane drawled, grim-mocking. "Sheriff Stroat an' his cabinet of scapegoat hunters." Dane's voice went hard, gruff with anger and menace. "Back against the wall, you birds! An' get your paws up where can see 'em!"

A ripple of movement swayed the watching men, and those five staring faces set like plaster as they shoved their empty hands ear-high.

"You brash young fool!" Stroat snarled. "You've thumbed your nose at the law once too often! You'll never —"

"Never is a right long time," Dane breathed. "Never mind me. Keep your mind on your *own* luck 'f you want to eat breakfast. Get back against that wall like I said."

Stroat's bitter stare was malignant with hatred. "By God, I've —"

"Just a minute," purred the man with the cigar stump jutting from his mouth. "What'll you take, young man, to quit this country — to put up that gun and get out of here?"

"I wouldn't quit now for all the cash in this country?"

"You know who I am, don't you?"

"Sure. You're Max Jackman — the guy

they're sayin' will be the next governor. But that don't mean nothin' to me. Get over against that wall with the rest —"

"I'll give you —"

"You're eyin' a gunfighter now that your money won't buy!"

The eyes beneath Jackman's frowning brows turned sharper. "What's there in this for you? What's Jupe Dolton to *you?*"

"Somethin' guys like you will never understand," Dane said bleakly. "It's your kind of man — your power and your money, that's pushed Jupe Dolton to where he is now. Never give a guy a break — that's your motto, ain't it?"

"Certainly not," Jackman said. "I've helped plenty young fellers. Dolton's different: a born crook and killer —"

"Yeah. I got a brother like Jupe. Mebbe you've heard of him. Bufe Telldane. He got his start same way Jupe's gettin' his — shoved into killin' by guys like you an' this scapegoat-huntin' sheriff here, Stroat! Now get back against that wall an' —"

The deputy had to try his luck. Dane's eye-corners caught the tag-end blur of his reaching hand; and his gun cracked once. The deputy dropped, cursing and groaning on the floor beside Frisby who froze in his tracks, features stiff, face gone wooden.

194

The others stood rocklike beside him.

Dane said: "Jupe — can you stand?"

Jupe tried but he couldn't make it. His weakened system was too exhausted. He fell against the chair and the chair skidded, dropping him, sprawling his length on the pounded-dirt floor.

The lampglow sharpened men's scowling faces; showed the hateful triumph that was twisting Stroat's. "You'll never cut it," he breathed vindictively. The hate and hope in him boiled through the silence; and the others leaned forward, hawk-eyed, watching, waiting. Waiting for Dane to try lifting Dolton.

The stillness became insupportably thin. Dane's shoulders hunched, slow lifted. "I'm takin' Jupe outa here, boys," he said quietly; and was easing forward, eyes bleak as agate, when a mutter of voices brushed in from outside. Dane Telldane stopped short.

Hake Rolsem's eyes blinked. Men were coming down the outside walk, their boots scuffing warning from the warped pine planks. Rolsem pivoted his big body, the glint of his eyes jumping doorward.

It was now or never.

"Jackman," Dane said, "throw Dolton across your shoulder."

Max Jackman grinned at him, enjoying this hugely. "I guess not. If you want him so bad, pick him up yourself."

The piled-up hush grew thick as clabber. They were all grinning now. They knew they had him.

Cold sweat beaded Dane's graven cheeks. With the tension clutching him like a jerkline he moved against Max Jackman, shoving against him solidly with his gun's hard muzzle digging into the man's soft belly. Forced to take his glance off the rest of them, Dane banked everything on Jackman's danger holding them motionless and brought the whole weight of his will against Jackman's nerve. "Ease around an' back over there by Jupe!"

Jackman's face showed damp but he stood like a rock.

Dane grew desperate. Suspense like a knife's edge rubbed his spine. The clatter of boots had gone still outside. A grumble of voice sound came through the door that connected this room with the bar — came toward it.

Dane said hoarsely: "I can only die once, Max. Make up your mind." And the knees nearly buckled under him in the rush of re-action when the cattle king, grunting, lurched abruptly round and, stooping, hoisted the prostrate Jupe to his shoulder. His eyes looked a question.

Gun ready, Dane said softly, "Rolsem, lock the barroom door," and saw big Hake stand dubious — saw his eyes dart a question at Stroat. But the sheriff refused the decision and, jowls quivering, Rolsem lumbered toward the door.

It burst open while his shaking hand was reaching for the key.

17

Come Hell or High Water

When Max Jackman had sent word to Cap Leigh, the United States Marshal, that events in the vicinity of Six-Shooter Siding showed a need for investigation — if not an actual and screaming cry for Federal intervention, Leigh was moved to reluctant action. It was not the policy of his superiors to meddle in local affairs of this kind, and Leigh would not have done so then had the request been voiced by another man. But Jackman was a power in the country, a man whose word could be completely trusted, and Leigh was confident the man would never have spoken if the need had not been great. The rancher was not the kind to make a mountain of a molehill; and another matter was urging Leigh to put a man in that country. Deke Straper, the one man sentenced thus far to life in the Santa Fe penitentiary, had recently escaped and was said to have been seen in the Sierra Negras, north of Tucumcari Mountain. So Leigh called in the best man under him and sent him posthaste to the Siding. That man was an expert, a fellow well fitted to cope with the gunfighter breed that had taken the country over. Leigh's instructions were brief and pointed. "I want Deke Straper. I want the man behind those train robberies. How you play this is up to you, *but don't come back without 'em.* I'll back you to the limit but I want that country cleaned!"

Kin Savvy overtook the girl without difficulty. He got a hold on her horse's bridle and pulled the bronco down to a walk. The girl was sobbing; she looked forlorn, miserable. Kin Savvy reached a hand to her shoulder gently. There was rare understanding in his tone. "Don't cry — the tears she's no good for time lak' thees. Some things a man mus' do, *muchacha* — no can help heemself. Thees Dane Telldane, she's all time help them underdog. I know hees brother — same way. No like for see eenjusteece."

But Dulcey would not listen. She drew away from him, sat huddled in her saddle as though her heart would break.

Kin Savvy said: "Don' you worry, *señorita.* That Dane, she's lucky hombre — plenty smart. No gon been made for keel that boy! She's save your brother sure.

Buck up: we mus' go for get the horses —"

A sound of gunfire clogged his speech.

Dulcey shuddered. The Mexican said urgently: "Queeck! We mus' get them caballos — he *depen'* on us!"

The words struck through fear's clutch of her, dissolving grief and panic to the urgent need for action. "You're right." She said it huskily; and brushing the tears from her cheeks she nodded. "You're a real friend to him. Do — do you really think he's a chance of making it?"

The Mexican shrugged. "Ees in the han's of God. We do w'at we can —"

"Yes!" Dulcey straightened. Snatched up her reins. "We must not fail him!"

But at the corral luck turned against them.

Pulled up in the deep-pooled shadows at the base of a giant pepper tree, they saw beyond the enclosure's slatted outline a knot of men, low-crouched and dark, with rifles ready to forestall the very attempt they had in mind.

Kin Savvy swore, cat-soft, in fluent Spanish. Dulcey's breath was a small stifled gasp as she followed the pointing of his lifted hand. Kin Savvy lowered it, eased the rifle from his stirrup fenders and silently laid it across his lap, keen eyes darkly questing the shadows. "Thees is bad," he muttered softly. "Jeez Chris', she's worst than that!"

"What can we do?" Dulcey's choked voice was an urgent whisper. The big Mex grunted, narrowed eyes still roving the gloom that might be hiding yet other men.

"If thees hombres —"

That much he said and bit the rest off, whirling, rifle lifted, bent forward as he stared uptown toward Rolsem's bar while the crouched night shook to the sudden crashing of pistols.

Dane knew, when he saw the knob turn, what was corning. The opening door spilled armed men toward him; and Rail Frisby shouted, *"Get 'im!"*

Dane fired point-blank and instantly into that huddle of startled gun-slicks — three shots; and his fourth knocked out the light in a clatter of fragmented glass that left the sheriff's jerked pistol blasting futile holes through a gun-ripped murk that was filled with fright and frenzy.

Even as darkness clutched the place Dane jumped and caught Jackman's shoulder. "This way!" he hissed, and shoved the cattle king doorwards — toward the door that gave on the alley. The rancher's outstretched hand found the latch and joggled it; his boot kicked the door, slamming it smashing against the outside wall as Dane dropped, dragging Jackman with him.

Every gun in the room seemed to blast its load at that gray rectangle left by the door.

Dane counted ten and came onto his feet, without mercy bringing his six-shooter down on the ranchman's shoulder as Jackman clawed for his gun. The cattle king, lurching, fell with a groan; and as he swayed aside Dane flung Jupe across his shoulder. That way, bent double under Dolton's weight, Dane reeled into the night, went crashing through the piles of cans that rolled and clanked and rattled beneath his stumbling feet, and were like king's trumpets in their blared announcements of his passage. And back there in the shout-torn murk Stroat's bull roar sailed blasphemous orders that went unheeded in the general pandemonium as man after man tripped snarling over the Territory's prospective next governor.

Panting, Dane turned a corner. Swinging round a building he ducked under a hitchrack and went lunging through the street's deep dust toward the corral that was at its end.

One thought hammered through his head. Were the Mex and the girl there waiting?

If they weren't —

He dared not think of that!

He shifted Jupe's weight to his other shoulder and was bending into his second wind when muzzle flame laid its glimmer across the forward gloom and a bullet's breath fanned his cheek. As though that shot were a signal all hell broke loose and the sound of lead was like hailstones all about him and the flash of exploding powder bit the gloom on every hand. Unseen fingers jerked at Dane's clothing, lead scraped his hide in at least three places and a heel was bludgeoned from one of his boots. Yet, miraculously, the blast left him standing — left him still on his feet and the feet still churning the dust of the road as he legged Jupe forward. Straight for the slatted shadows of the pole corral he lunged; for it was there that he'd ordered Kin Savvy to meet him — to meet him with Dulcey and fresh saddled horses. And he'd get there by God come high water or hell!

18

Strong Medicine

Then, abruptly, new sound clouted that roaring din — the sharp *crackcrack* of a high-powered rifle. Out of that yonder tree gloom it burst; and with it, over it, through and above it high-yipping, derisive, came Kin Savvy's loud shout: "Geef it to them! Boys — *dab eet on them!*"

Bedlam broke from the pole corral. Black blobs of shadow, the silhouetted shapes of frantic men, came ducking under and clambering over that pen's peeled bars; stumbling, fumbling, fiddle-footed in their terror, squealing and scuttling like harried jack rabbits. And the big Mex's taunting laugh sailed after them, mocking them as he worked his rifle.

"Thees way, amigo!"

Telldane veered, while back of him the sheriff's hired guns redoubled their efforts to bring him down. Lead batted the hat chin-strapped to his throat, sliced at his vest — made the trip a nightmare; but he stumbled on, determined to make it. And reaching hands lifted Dolton's weight from his shoulders; and from his other side came Dulcey's fervent "Dane? Thank God!"

Telldane cuffed the hat from his eyes and found her; found them all beneath a pepper's curdled gloom with the big Mex lifting Jupe into a saddle. Dane grabbed up Kin Savvy's rifle, found it loaded. Maliciously he whirled and emptied it, scattering Stroat's gun-slicks, driving them to cover.

"By grab," he said, "mebbe that'll learn 'em! Did you get fresh broncs?" he snapped at Kin Savvy.

The Mex shook his head. "Thees Stroat, she's have men cached in corral — gone now. You get —"

"You'll come with me or we cash this here!"

Kin Savvy shrugged and they broke from cover, streaking across the emptied street; Jupe and the girl still mounted, Dane and Kin Savvy low-crouched alongside, each with a hand hard-clamped to a stirrup. Around the far side of the pen they lunged while the horses enclosed there shied, milled and snorted their fear of this raucous turmoil. Through the bars, hot and breathless, the two men scrambled, ropes in hand, nooses twirling. "Bronc apiece!"

Dane gritted; and the ropes snaked out, each loop flicked true to the neck of a horse. . . . They snatched saddles from a kak-pole and while they worked Dulcey sprayed the dark street with Kin Savvy's rifle.

"Where now?"

"I dunno," Telldane panted. A weary gesture pawed the sweat from his eyes. "The ranch is out. Stroat'll look there first —"

"She'll no look, by Chris', for them Black Jack's rancho!"

"Are you daffy?" Dane growled.

But the big Mex chuckled. "No one be there," he said with conviction. "Two weeks ago them Ketchum's stick up stage in Steins Pass country. Rob one bank an' —"

"How do *you* know that?"

"Kin Savvy smart — sabe plenty. Them Black Jack an' Sam, she's rob thees place before — get brash lak' hell! Ten days ago they rob store at Bell ranch; load up wagon — vamose! I'm hear all about eet. Thees Stroat, she's don't sabe nothings. Beeg fight out there at them Ketchum rancho — they 'ave stuck up Hernstein place at Liberty. Hernstein get bunch of Mexican boys — raid Ketchum for get stuff back. No get!

Hernstein killed — three-four other guys. Them Ketchums, she's clear out — be gone, you bet! Ranch empty now; good place for hide."

Telldane stared at him bleakly.

"Better we go, eh?" Kin Savvy grinned. "Go queeck — get the hell out of here!"

"By grab," Dane said, "I sure can't figure you. Where'd you find out all that stuff? What is this — another damn trap?"

"No trap. *Válgame Dios* — thees ees truth! I'm find out plenty when I'm work for them Black Jack. Jeez Chris'! I'm bes' finder-outer in whole damn' co'ntry!"

Telldane snorted. "If you know so much, where's Ketchum's gang now?"

"Near 'Lizabethtown — forted up in the mountains. Get ready for hold up D. & F. W. railroad — Señor 'Arrington's train. Stick 'em up at Folsom —"

"I'll be damned!" Dane said, and whipped up his reins. "We better telegraph —"

"No telegraph. Thees fella you mention — thees guy, Deke Straper — she's telegraph man at Siding. Teep 'em off —"

"Then we better find Stroat —"

Dane was wheeling his horse when the Mex grabbed his bridle. "Hold on! Thees Stroat, she's no leesten —"

"By God we'll make him listen!" Dane

207

cried fiercely. "You've got dope enough to clear Jupe completely! If half what you say is true —"

"It's true, all right; but you can't tell thees Stroat — She's be too bullheaded. She's shoot you full of holes like sieve! Use the head, amigo. We go for ranch, leave Jupe an' girl. You an' me then, by Chris', we do somet'ings! We go by Folsom — ketch them Black Jack when she's rob the train! Eh? How you like the sound for that?"

"By grab," Dane said, "it's ideal, boy!"

19

"If You Want It That Way —"

But it was not to be as swift as that.

Jupe had come to before Kin Savvy finished and he didn't like the program any — in particular his part of it as outlined by the Mexican. "Hell's hinges!" he was grumbling. "Just because I've lost a mite of blood ain't no reason for countin' me outa things. If what this whippoorwill just said is so, then I want in on it! I got a damn' sight bigger score with that tribe than any of you an' I sure as hell ain't gonna —"

"Quiet!" Dane said. "There's somebody poundin' the valley road!" And they sat their saddles, stiffly listening, while the braver of Stroat's scattered posse began a cautious sniping from retaken positions. But the drum of hoofs could be heard all right. A body of horsemen was coming fast.

"By gar," Kin Savvy cried, "I'm think we better go!"

But already the time was past when they could slip away. Stroat held the north of town and all the trails leading out of it; and from the valley road, sheering in past Tucumcari Mountain, came a compact huddle of low-bent riders whose rifles gleamed in the faint star haze.

Kin Savvy, swearing softly, lifted the Winchester across his saddle and even Jupe got an extra Colt from one of his boots and, with a gun in each fist, was cocked to fire when Dane said:

"Wait! Let's play this careful! Whoever that is they're not *our* friends — but maybe they'll serve us. Back in the shadows — quick! Here they come."

Full tilt into town swept the unknown horsemen. They had seen Dane's party slide into the shadows. They set their broncos straight back on their haunches and the boss of the outfit yelled through Stroat's firing: "*Quién es? Quién es?* Sing out or we'll drop you!"

The voice was Luce Jackman's.

Dane, with his tones gruffened up and different, called: "Hold your fire — we're a part of Stroat's posse!"

"Who's that firin' up yonder? Where's Stroat?"

"Stroat's dead. That's Ketchum's outfit — they're lootin' the town —"

"The goddam fools!" Jackman's voice

ripped out. He whirled his horse, but stopped when one of his men said something. Dane could see his head tip down; could feel the sharpness of his stare. Jackman called: "Come over here! I want —"

"Hell's hinges!" Jupe snarled. "What'd you wanta tell him that for? Now we're —"

"I'm handlin' this!" Dane snapped. "Get a hold on your jaw an' back my play." He lifted his voice: "Is that you, Jackman?"

"Sure it's me! Get over here 'fore I blast —"

"You ain't talkin' to your own pelados —"

"Them Stroat," Kin Savvy's tone was urgent, "she's sneak for make the surround — *see?* Queeck, amigo! We got for hustle!"

Stroat's men had been quick to take advantage of this parley and were deploying as the Mexican had said. Swift-flitting figures stealthily dodging, swift-ducking vague shapes that were stretching a circle.

Rail Frisby's bull bellow rang the night like a tocsin. "Jackman! Luce Jackman! That's Dolton's gang — *stop 'em!*"

Dane bent in the saddle and thumbed swift shots above Jackman's riders, striving to throw them into confusion and hold them witless in the street until his own crowd could get among them and be screened from the posse's bullets; and back of him a gun began to lay flat, spanging waves of sound through the raucous town, and he knew Kin Savvy had unlimbered the Winchester. But Jupe cursed, furious. "You goddam fools! These boys are our friends!" Raging, he drove his horse full into Dane's, his slashing arm trying to knock Dane's gun down. But Dane shied clear, loosed another quick shot and saw Jackman's crew go up in the air on pitching broncs they could not fight down. Then all was an uproar, wild dinning confusion.

Dane pulled a long breath into his lungs. "Jupe! Kin Savvy! Dulcey — quick! Into 'em! Through 'em! It's our only chance!" He raked his bronc with flashing rowels and the big bay whirled, lunged out from the shadows; and the other broncs followed pounding hard at his heels.

They entered the road at a rocketing gallop and Stroat's posse rose up and went mad with their rifles, flinging bursts of sound crashing through the night. Every doorframe and window showed a red-tongued challenge and the air was filled with its shrilling whistle; but Dane Telldane neither swerved nor faltered, and his horse leaped swift toward that huddle of riders. One among them suddenly whirled clear and fired and that lead laid its track against Telldane's cheek.

Dane yelled, "Hold your fire!" then was in among them with that one whirled-free rider still working his trigger, maliciously determined to cut someone down. Dane's guiding knee shoved the bay to the left, trying to reach this man, but a horseman cut between them and other riders joggled them together and Dane, gone desperate, emptied the fellow from his saddle with one down-slicing slash of his gun barrel. The roaring pistol flamed again, the flash of its muzzle light leaping toward him, the whole night seeming to rock with that close report as Dane swayed aside with sweat breaking across his forehead and all his nerves constricted and the pit of his belly gone drum tight.

The fool seemed wild to get him a victim and Dane's mind, razor-sharp, wondered which among Jackman's crew was turned traitor. Then the man's gun roared again right in front of Dane and the man's voice shouted: *"Jupe! Jupe, goddam you, where the hell are you?"* and Dane's lifted hammer clicked down on an empty shell; and other riders broke in between them and Dane lost the fellow. Lost him — but he could not forget that voice; he thought he never should forget it. And if he ever got his hands —

Anger ripped through him in ragged streaks that reached clear down to his finger tips, and for seconds that whole churning maelstrom of tossing riders went black before his vision. Then he fought it down and threw all that aroused, savage energy into getting clear of these Jackman riders. And then he *was* clear, and the others with him; and they went tearing down the starlit trail at a hard wild run that put the gun sound back of them, finally losing the pulse of it utterly.

Minutes later Jupe rammed his horse up alongside Dane's. "What the hell were you shootin' at Jackman's crowd for? Tryin' to lose me the last friend I've got?"

"The last friend you've got is yourself, Dolton," Dane said. Then, less gruffly: "Unless you're countin' Kin Savvy an' me."

Jupe snarled: "What's the meanin' of that?" He crowded his horse against Dane's horse, slowing both mounts to a walk. "More of yore goddam riddles?" He said: "I'm tired of your high-handed ways! You answer me straight —"

"If you want it that way, you can have it. Luce Jackman's no friend of yours — that was him that was usin' that pistol."

20

What a Man Has to Do

Kin Savvy, jogging alongside, growled: "You know w'at I'm theenk?"

"Yes," Dane said, "I'm thinkin' the same myself." And he kicked his bay to a faster gait, being more than fed up with Jupe's humors. It was not at all hard to see why young Dolton had been chosen scapegoat for the things going on in his country. The wonder was that with his unstable temper Jupe had kept clear of the noose this long.

In what few moments Dane had for thinking, he had given his mind to Jupe's problems; and, more and more, those problems were taking simple and definite shape. Jupe was a distinct product of his environment; no other thing — unless it were his temper — so surely had molded and shaped him. Born and bred to this land of turbulence, turbulence was in him; it was the driving power that moved him and would be, like enough, what killed him when his number came up on the board. It was Jupe's answer to every argument, to every obstacle and pressure.

It was the gunfighter way.

How well Dane knew it! More often than not it was his way, too; and he scowled at the swirling shadows, reflecting that — like Jupe — he would probably go out with his boots on. Yet why the thought should be so bitter he could not say, save that, some way, it was tied up with Jupe's sister. He had never tried to analyze his feelings toward the girl, and did not try now. It was the crazy pattern of events holding this country in its grip that, so doggedly, was challenging his energies. For there *was* a pattern, and a sinister one; and he sensed that somewhere back of it was a malign, very human, agency.

Some man or men were behind Jupe Dolton's disasters — behind these things that had befallen Rafter; were framing them of deliberate purpose that would not be served till the last Dolton alive had been driven from the land.

But *why?*

Dane was certain the Rock Island pay rolls — though a plenty in themselves — were but chicken feed to the baleful influence that had steeped this land in violence. They were not the end — just a means to an end; the end was something blacker, something many times more coveted than a handful of gun-snatched dollars. Why had Sprawley Clark been killed? Surely that was no isolated incident, but a part and parcel of the whole dark aim, like the killing of Jupe's father — like the fright that had killed his mother.

And Stroat: what part had the Quay County sheriff in this scheme for stealing a family's birthright? For it was Rafter they were after; Dane was sure enough of that. Was Stroat what he seemed — a gruff and blundering officer? an unwitting tool like Jupe and Ketchum? Or was he something darker — the directing genius of these things that were writing Quay County history?

Dane could not say, any more than he could say what thing had clamped Luce Jackman's finger —

"*Mira* — look," Kin Savvy softly called. "We are there, amigo. Thees place up wonder, she's belong to them Ketchum. See? Ees lak I say — close op; them Black Jack gone."

The place did indeed appear deserted. Dim-seen through the shadows, untouched by the moon's risen splendor, a shack's gaunt lines showed vaguely from the tree gloom; and off to one side, where the night's dark held less density, was an empty pole corral.

Dane pulled the bay down to a cat-footing walk and raised a hand for silence while he quartered the place with a raking stare, having well in mind that other trap this Mex had led them into.

But the Ketchum headquarters seemed emptied of care; not even a dog barked challenge, and no movement showed anywhere in the yard but was stirred by the wind off the mountains.

Dane nodded, satisfied, and kneed the big bay forward. They were almost at the gate when the bay's ears dropped flat against his head and he shied back, snorting.

Dane slid to the ground, gun out and lifted. *"Quién es?"* he demanded sharply, but only the echoes gave answer and he said with a thin, banked challenge: "Kin Savvy! Strike a match!"

A match head rasped and a tiny flame sprang up in the Mex's cupped hands. It showed a dark, still blotch on the trail ahead and yonder, to the left, another.

Kin Savvy breathed through his nose a kind of sigh and said: "Thees dead mans. You recall? I tol' you the Liberty store man, Hernstein —"

"Never mind the yarn," Telldane said sharply. "An' keep your hands away from that belt. What I'm honin' to know is how you come to be so well posted."

The Mex spread his hands in a Latin shrug, teeth flashing in the starlight. "Ees simple. I 'ave talk to Placido Chaves who was come here weeth Hernstein for catch them Black Jack. You see" — he waved an all-encompassing arm — "no have moch luck, thees fellow. Hernstein kill'. Two Mexican, she's kill too. Them Black Jack pull the freight."

"Don't they bury their dead?" Jupe growled at him.

"Them Black Jack, she's no have dead, Placido say. All dead, Hernstein. You look."

"No, thanks," Jupe muttered, and got laboriously out of his saddle while Kin Savvy opened the gate.

They were ready to set out upon the trail to Folsom, and Kin Savvy had the rested horses saddled, when Dulcey followed Dane from the shack, put a hand out clutching his arm. "Dane —"

He faced her, frozen, wordless.

Jupe was in the house in a bunk, well wrapped in a blanket, fed, fresh-bandaged, asleep and comfortable as a man could be who had used himself so sorely. It was not for Jupe, that light in her eyes; and Dane stood moveless, knowing.

The hold of her fingers tightened.

In sudden anguish he said: "Dulcey, I've got —"

"I know. I know," she said, and her words were like a judgment. "You've got to do what a man always has — you've got to be in the thick of it." She said with sudden bitterness: "I wish I were a man!" Then her voice dropped dully, turned listless. "You'll be busy, Dane; things will move too fast for thought. I think this country's hardest on a woman. Always we're left behind with the dragging hours and —"

"Dulcey —"

"Sh-h! I know. You are a man."

She brushed a hand across his cheeks, feeling them as a blind person might, trying to etch their shape in her memory.

Something happened to him then. He pulled her to him, kissed her, humbly — felt her arms creep round him. She clung to him as though never, never would she let him go; and he saw how her eyes were closed and the long brown lashes lay against her cheeks, and he closed his own, shutting out the waiting horses.

That one moment was theirs. For all eternity it belonged to them, and was stamped indelibly upon their memories.

With a little moan she broke away; and with his eyes still closed he heard her running, heard the rustling of her skirts. The slamming of the screen door left him in a world gone empty. Cold and stark . . .

Fit place for the gunfighter breed.

21

Hard Lines

This was a high, wild land through which the horses were taking them. They had been riding without pause since sunup and it was now well into the night, and still they rode, ever bearing northward. Through the Sierra Negras and the *de los Comancheros* they had come and, following the twists of Ute Creek, had skirted the San Carlos Hills. In the broken country then they swung northeasterly between the frowning ramparts of Laughlin's Peak and Palo Blanco. It was ten o'clock by the moon and the stars and they had just crossed Carrizo Creek.

"Just whereabouts is this Folsom Station?" Dane spoke out of a long, long silence.

"On Cimarron," Kin Savvy grunted, "een the mountains near Emerys Peak — we be there five-six hours." He stretched a hand toward the two great peaks that reared rugged cones against the sky. "Antelope — *Sierra Grande.*" He gave it the tone of an introduction; and Dane looked across at him slantways.

It was odd, uncommon odd, he thought, the way this Mex in his brush-clawed finery was able to flip out answers. There seemed to be one on his tongue for every question, and not once had Dane caught him napping. Kin Savvy, he called himself, which meant in the lingo "Who Knows."

The man was a mystery — baffling. With his half-moon face and black mustache, his flashing teeth and his shrugs, he was the perfect soldier of fortune, a drifter come out of nowhere and going to the same place in a hurry. Casually, during the ranchward flight from the corral fight, Dane had mentioned the fellow he'd met on the trail who so greatly resembled Deke Straper; and the Mex had shown a veiled interest. Last night Dane had mentioned meeting the man in town with Morg Trotter, and Kin Savvy had only shrugged. Yet, later, when Dane had suggested telegraphing Jack Ketchum's plans to Santa Fe or some other place where authorities might be interested, Kin Savvy had shaken his head emphatically, declaring Deke Straper was telegraph man at the Siding and would promptly tip Ketchum off. But he'd said things a sight more startling than that —

his knowledge of Ketchum's plans was un-canny. One minute he was convinced the Mex was a member of Ketchum's gang; the next he was equally certain the man couldn't be. It sure had Dane fighting his hat.

If the man intended explaining himself he would do so in his own good time; there was no use trying to question him. But one thing Dane was resolved to do; he meant to watch the man like a hawk. Dane was in this to clear Dulcey's brother who he was thoroughly convinced was innocent of the things charged against him; so long as Kin Savvy backed that play he might remain mysterious as he pleased.

The Mex seemed to sense Dane's covert scrutiny, for he laughed, wheeling round in his saddle. "Let the breath out, amigo," he chuckled. "Kin Savvy, she's no try for ron away."

Dane snorted softly. "Got a line on them palominos yet?"

The big Mex grinned mysteriously. "Better we stop for w'ile. Rest the caballos, eh? Take mebbe five hours for get Folsom. No rosh. Plenty time — train not due be-fore tomorrow night. Mebbeso we take the nap, eh?"

Dane was not averse. They pulled the

gear from their horses, rubbed the animals down and hobbled them. With a tiny fire between them they spread their blankets and turned in, each man facing the other with a pistol handy, each man elaborate in his paraded indifference to the fact. Kin Savvy chatted garrulously and sleepily for quite a spell, then finally rolled up in his blanket and went immediately to sleep.

Or so it seemed.

The fire burned low, and for dragging hours the noise of crickets was the only sound in the mountain stillness. Then the Mex stirred softly, came up on an elbow — and found Dane movelessly regarding him across a leveled six-gun.

The moon's blue light showed Kin Savvy's lips stretched across his teeth in a grin. "By gar," he said, "I'm damn near forget for tell you good night, amigo. *Buenas noches,*" he chuckled, and curled back down in his blanket.

It was eight o'clock the next morning when they rode into Folsom flagstop. They found the hamlet boiling, seething with rancor and rumor. Conductor Harrington's passenger train, on its southbound run to Fort Worth, had been stopped and robbed there several days previous. It was the Ketchum gang. They had pulled the job ahead of time.

22

"We Better Meet It —"

Kin Savvy looked stunned when they told him.

He stood there in the bright sunlight with the look of a man on the thirteenth step. He could not seem to believe it — seemed determined *not* to believe it. But the evidence was beyond man's blinking. One of the passengers, a coffee drummer who'd been on the train, was in the crowd. He told a story pungently detailed.

Kin Savvy groaned. He walked stiff-legged to the tiny depot and dropped down onto a bench. There seemed not a grin left in him.

"By God," he said. "An' to think — to think how I let that wolf bamboozle me . . . The lyin' hound! It's enough —"

He quit abruptly, eyes flashing at Dane. Dane, with his own gaze slitted and thin, said: "Go on — finish it. Where'd you pick up the education? What's happened to your fine Mex lingo?"

But Kin Savvy's quick-glinting grin

didn't come, nor his customary glib explanation. He groaned again, jammed hands in his pockets and cursed with a wealth of feeling. He dragged a morose hand across his face and glared at his boot tops. "Of all the rotten lousy luck — an' just when I had the thing cinched!"

"I'm listenin'," Dane reminded. "I got a great capacity for learnin'." He tapped his holstered six-gun. "Cut loose, hombre, an' start unravelin', or me an' you is due to tangle."

Kin Savvy dragged the chin from his chest. His regard of Dane was the sort of look a man might give a pestiferous gadfly he was debating the chances of swatting. He sat that way for some moments, abruptly grunting. With a semblance of his old Latin shrug he took the right fist from his pocket. Dane stared when he opened his fingers.

A badge lay on the rope-scarred palm; fancy, bright with embossing. *The badge of a deputy marshal.*

The implications snatched Dane's breath away. Then he said, contrarily resentful: "So that tale about them Rancho Grande horses was just a pile of hogwash? Like I suspected! Like that paper with them highfalutin seals you got tucked inside your shirt there!"

"*Pues, no, amigo* — you 'ave jomp to the — w'at you say? — gonclusions." Kin Savvy's old smile flashed a moment, went twisted and died. "Ah — God!" he said. "An' I come so near to cuttin' it!"

For a little longer Dane eyed him. Then, "You know where you can go," he said, and turned on his heel. But Kin Savvy growled: "Don't quit me now — by grab, I'm needin' you a damn' sight worse than Jupe is. Come back here, pard — come back an' set down. I'm goin' to swing some chin music; an' when I'm done, you give me the answer."

Dane took an edge of the bench with his lean face still suspicious.

But the big Mex marshal's tale was simple, straightforward; graphic and clear beyond all doubting.

A complaint and a plea had been handed to Leigh's office by no less a person than Maxwell Jackman. This country, Max had declared, was being overrun with thieves and killers. The Rock Island's transcontinental tracks — on which the Territory was banking for its share of immigration — were in grave danger of being stopped for good just north of Tucumcari Mountain. They had lost six pay rolls in the last three months and Frisby's section hands were quitting. Stages were being stopped, posts robbed and cow towns raided. The country was filled with unrest and turmoil — no man's life was safe. It was time — past time, Jackman said, that the Marshal's office did something.

Cap Leigh, the marshal, hard pressed on the same score from other quarters, had called Kin Savvy in off a rustling case he'd been investigating at Shiprock. Just as Kin Savvy had been ready to take over, word had come from the Rurales at Agua Prieta of the mysterious theft of the Rancho Grande palominos. The Mexican authorities had reason to believe these horses had gone into the Tucumcari country and had requested help from the United States marshal. Enclosed with their request were papers and a warrant signed in blank. It was this warrant Kin Savvy had shown Dane. Kin Savvy — on a mission for the Texas Rangers once — had been down in that country and had seen the palominos. To Cap Leigh the Rurales' request and warrant had looked like a godsend, providing his man with a cover for being in that country; and he had sent the big Mex off at once. "Your job," Leigh had told him, "is to get Deke Straper and the man behind those train robbings. I don't care how you do it, but don't come back without 'em! I want that country cleaned!"

The rest of Kin Savvy's tale was similar to what he had already told Dane; about how he'd gone to Ketchum's spread, been suspected and barely gotten clear with his life. His yarn about the pact between himself and Stroat had been substantially correct. But there were one or two other things he hadn't previously told Dane.

It was while he was working for Ketchum that he'd overheard the details of the Steins Pass job and Bell Ranch robbery; and the very afternoon before Ketcham jumped him he had discovered them laying pipe to stop Conductor Harrington's train at Folsom.

"Sure," Dane said; "that was why Jack Ketchum jumped you. They were wise to you —"

"By gar, I'll swear they weren't!" declared Kin Savvy with conviction. "Oh, they were wise to me all right so far as knowing I was up to something. But they sure hadn't tumbled to me overhearing their plans to stop that train — they *couldn't* have! I —"

"Then I reckon they changed their minds," Dane said, "an' decided to stick it up sooner."

Though neither Dane nor Kin Savvy was aware of it that was exactly what had happened. While the outlaws were holed up in the hills waiting for the rains to bring spring grass so that they would not be hampered in their getaway by having to pack feed, Black Jack and Sam had got into a heated argument. Jack in a rage had ridden off, telling them they could rob their train and be damned, that he would not have any part in it: that he was going back to Texas and quit the goddam trade. It was after Black Jack had gone that the gang made up their minds to stop old Harrington sooner.

Kin Savvy eyed Dane dubiously. "Mebbe so," he said. "But the question is, what am I going to do about it? Those birds have prob'ly scattered now to hell-an'-gone."

"You know where Straper is," Dane mentioned. "You can grab *him* anyway. Have you a line on those palominos?"

"No — worse luck! I know plenty well Ketchum's outfit got 'em. But I ain't seen 'em. I could never —"

"Never," Dane said dryly, "is a mighty parcel of time, boy. Let me think a minute."

Kin Savvy fell silent, morose and brooding, long-faced.

Dane's head tipped up. "Ever notice how Ketchum's crowd always larrups around on black horses? Kind of a mangy off-color — Hell!" Dane cried excitedly. "That bronc you're ridin' is the one I grabbed off Trotter — Come here!"

Kin Savvy, slightly more animated now, followed him over to the ground-hitched horses. Dane was spitting on the shoulder of Trotter's bronc and roughly scrubbing the place with his knuckles. It *did* look a mite less black than the rest of his soot-colored hide. "I'm bettin' that's just what the dang stuff is, too — soot!" Dane said with conviction.

He swung up into his saddle. "C'mon," he growled. "We'll damn quick learn!"

He lined off for the river; and Kin Savvy, without enthusiasm, followed. Water, a few hatfuls slopped on the horse, proved Dane right beyond any doubting.

"He don't show yellow yet," Dane said, "but he will if he's scrubbed enough. The Ketchum gang's ridin' your palominos!"

"All of which," Kin Savvy said, "ain't gettin' 'em back for us, hombre."

"All we got to do," Dane grinned, "is to get our hands on that outfit —"

"Yeah!" There were no grins left in Kin Savvy. He was bitter and plainly disgusted.

"Stick around," Dane said. "I'll be right back. I'm goin' to find out somethin'," he added, and rode off in the direction of town.

He was back inside the hour, and some contour of his expression made Kin Savvy slim his eyes down. "What's up? You get a line on 'em?"

"No," Dane said. "But Harrington's train is due back tonight. I got a hunch we better meet it."

23

"As Sure as Hell's Hot!"

They decided to go back up in the hills a way and camp till it got near train time. It was better not to arouse suspicion; and two strangers loafing around where the town's few residents could see them would be sure to cause comment — perhaps trouble. Folsom wasn't fond of gents with a talent for stopping trains, and in its present mood a stranger was likely to remain healthy longer if he kept out of sight.

But time was like cold molasses.

Dane and Kin Savvy took turns dozing, but they were in no mood for sleep and finally they quit trying.

"The trouble with your job," Dane said, "is it's got too many loose ends. You can say what you will, but I'm bettin' anything you care to name there's a nigger hidin' back of Jack Ketchum."

Kin Savvy looked a question.

"What I mean," Dane growled, "is there's somebody smarter than Jack or Sam that's pullin' the strings to this business. Think it over. You're not pushin' enough weight to the Dolton angle."

Kin Savvy wrinkled up his nose. He looked thoughtful. "Unload it, hombre."

Dane said: "It strikes me that Ed Dolton's murder was the start of the whole blame business. The pay-roll stick-ups came after —"

"Only because there wasn't any track laid down this far when Jupe's old man got rubbed out."

"Un-uh." Dane shook his head. "That's an angle, but it ain't the right one. The pay-roll stick-ups was outgrowths of Ed Dolton's killin'. They was by way o' bein' afterthoughts."

"If that's your idea of bein' entertainin' —"

"I'm here," Dane growled, "to help you —"

"Pipe dreams ain't goin' to help me any. Do you realize how much dinero them stick-ups been knockin' down each crack?"

"Chicken feed," Dane said, and muttered: "The fellow that's ribbed up this sideshow is after the real mazuma; I'll bet you he's throwin' every cent of that Rock Island money to Ketchum Brothers an' Company just to keep 'em rakin' chestnuts —"

"Rakin' chestnuts!" Kin Savvy snorted. "If I sprung that stuff on the Marshal, boy, he'd swear I been smokin' rattleweed. Nope — it won't hold water, fella. I'd like to believe you — like to help you out; but there's some things only a whale could swaller —"

Dane, hunkered on his heels, grunted. "Just the same," he muttered doggedly, "you'll have to admit my notion's got a heap of backin'. The way I dope it out, Ed Dolton's murder, Sprawley Clark's killin', the train stick-ups an' all Jupe's rotten luck is part an' parcel of the same damn pattern —"

"What pattern?"

"The scheme to get some slick guy's hooks jabbed into Dolton's Rafter."

Kin Savvy grinned at Dane skeptically. "I suppose you *are* tryin' to be helpful," he said, "but —"

"Haul up," Dane growled, "an' look the figures over. The Ketchum boys come driftin' into this country from over Arizona way where they been playin' at bein' tough in the Steins Pass country. Shortly after they show up here Jupe's father gets rubbed out one night within six miles of their boundary. Meantime, on Ketchum evidence, Sheriff Stroat shows up at the Rafter with a warrant for Jupe that's been issued on a charge of cattle rustlin'. Jupe digs for the tules an' Stroat gets the owl-hoot brand put on him. The Rock Island starts losin' pay rolls an' word gets round that Jupe is bossin' a wild bunch. The Rafter foreman is murdered — would Jupe, d'you think, pull that stunt? The Rafter hands ride in an' ask for their time, forthwith quittin' the country. An' that ain't natural, either — I say them fellows been bought. Bought an' bribed out of the country. But no matter! Miz Dolton hires on a busted-down wrangler from Logan or some place, an' five-six mornin's later one of Luce Jackman's crew finds this fella with a broke neck down in the bottom of a gulch."

"Sounds good," Kin Savvy said, non-committally.

"Good, eh? Well, it's got a polecat smell to me," Dane said. "An' that ain't all by a jugful! The Rafter's got a bad rep now — there ain't a man that'll risk ridin' for it. Jupe's mother an' sister are left on the spread alone — I forgot to mention that just before Ed's murder the Rafter headquarters ranch was burned to the ground — plumb gutted. So the women are livin' at one of the line camps. All by their lonesome. That was the picture when I stepped into it. Jupe on the dodge, an' them two women there by themselves."

Kin Savvy stared at him. Waited.

"But somethin'," Dane said, "had happened there just before I shoved into it. Jupe had come back and Ketchum had been in to see Stroat with a complaint. Ketchum told the sheriff Jupe had raided his ranch, set fire to a couple of the buildin's an' killed the Ketchum cook — claimed they saw Jupe's face in the flame light. What actually happened was, Jupe had been watchin' Ketchum's place through the glasses an' had seen his crowd ride out. It was Jupe's hunch they were on their way to another train stick-up and he followed them. When it got dark he made camp an' took up the trail soon as day come. He run smack into their camp and lit out in a hail of lead. After that Jupe don't know where they went, but they was headin' towards the railroad when he lost 'em. He decided to go home an' see his womenfolks. Two hours after he got back to the ranch, Jack Ketchum rode in with his crew — you should know, you was with 'em. He tried to rub Jupe out, but Jupe got clear. Point is, Ketchum threw rifle fire into that shack, knowin' them two women was in there. Don't that mean nothin' to you?"

Softly the big Mex marshal swore. "It's beginnin' to," he muttered.

"It ought to," Dane said. "I rode into town for supplies next mornin' an' made proclamation I was roddin' the Rafter — thought mebbe it would put a brake on the rough stuff." He grimaced, recalling what it *had* done. "Then you quit Ketchum an' showed up at the Sidin' in time for us to get acquainted — havin' in the meantime made a crazy deal with Stroat. That deal musta made the Big Guy chuckle. They used you, boy, hopin' to trap Jupe Dolton proper. But it didn't work out that way; so Stroat grabbed onto Jupe's sister. That tooled Jupe into town an' Stroat grabbed him. I sprung him loose an' here we are. But what I'm tryin' to show you is — every step of the way, all this hell raisin' centers round the owners of the Rafter! I say, by God someone's out to get that ranch!"

For a long time Kin Savvy squatted there, staring down into the line of green that marked the course of the Cimarron. Then he looked up and shook his head. "It's not enough."

"You don't believe it, eh?"

"Most of it, yeah — but not your conclusions. You see everything in terms of Jupe Dolton —"

"That's the only way *to* see it!" Dane snapped. "Why do you suppose Sprawley

Clark was killed? An' all them things of Jupe's planted there?"

Kin Savvy shrugged. "I'm listenin'."

"Sprawley Clark," Dane said, "was known to be Black Jack Ketchum's woman. Get it?" He tapped the big marshal's knee. "She was known to be Black Jack's woman — and Jupe Dolton had been playin' round with her! Why? Because he was huntin' for information! He figured Black Jack might of let somethin' slip an' he was pumpin' Sprawley Clark to find out! That's why she was killed!"

"To shut her mouth?" Very soft the big Mex said it. "You think Black Jack put that knife —"

"Black Jack," Dane growled, "was not a talkin' man. He was the kind that keeps his mouth shut. But Jupe was desperate. Pumpin' Sprawley looked like a chance, an' he was workin' it for all he was able. Which wasn't much because Stroat had got wise he was seeing her an' was havin' her watched —"

"You think Stroat killed her? Hell! the fellow's too fool —"

"Stroat didn't kill her," Dane said. "Nor Black Jack either. Stroat was havin' her mighty close watched —"

"Then how could *any*one —"

241

"The man that plunged that knife in Sprawley was somebody Stroat knew — somebody Stroat's deputies knew. Somebody," Dane said grimly, "this whole stretch of country knows too well to ever suspect or even *think* of doubtin'. Some guy that's got the run of the range —"

"Jackman!"

Dane's nod plumbed the depths of gloom. "Like scratchin' your ear with your elbow; but that's who I got in mind."

Kin Savvy sat on his boot heels frozen, dumbstruck by the implications. The mountain stillness crept up round them, and still Kin Savvy squatted there, his face gone darkly wooden as the carving of some santo. Only his eyes showed life. Bright they were — gunbarrel-bright, with the swiftness of his thoughts.

"If you can prove —"

"Ask for a miracle an' be done with it. I told you it would be like scratchin' your ear with your elbow." Dane, picking up a stick, made aimless markings in the sand. "If I could prove — Hell's fire! If I could I'd not be passin' it on to you. Right here," he growled, slapping hand against holster, "is all the law I'd ask for." He pulled a last drag from his cigarette, sent it pin-wheeling into the rocks. "An' off-hand I'd say it will come to that."

He got up with hands jammed into his pockets and took one bleak turn round the clearing. "If he gets his way she'll have to go — like Jupe, an' Jupe's dad, an' Jupe's mother. The man's —"

"I thought —" Kin Savvy broke in, and shrugged. "If you're right — if Jackman's our man — how come him to be so set on gettin' Jupe arrested?"

"Didn't know he was," Dane said. "Must be a play for the record. Doesn't make much difference. Jupe wouldn't never get no trial; they'd never das' chance him oratin'. Necktie'd be cheaper an' a sight more savin' on the wear an' tear to folks' nerves. Particularly Jackman's." Dane said explosively: "It's Jackman, sure as hell's hot!"

24

Folsom Flagstop

It was dark in the oak brush bordering the track near Folsom flagstop. The two friends, with their horses tied behind them, squatted cowboy-fashion on their boot heels while they waited for Harrington's train. The big Mex marshal didn't think much of the chances; was inclined to regard Dane's hunch as having kept them here for a goose hunt. As the cold wind rattled the leaves of the scrubby timber Dane grew more than half convinced Kin Savvy was right. The long day's inaction had turned him morose and gloomy; Ketchum's gang would never be such fools as to rob the same train twice, hand-running. And if he were right in suspecting Jackman of being the man behind this country's troubles, what might not the fellow be up to now with Dulcey left at Ketchum's ranch unguarded? To be sure, Jupe was there; but he was not in shape to offer much resistance. If Jackman found them —

Kin Savvy jogged Dane's elbow. "She's a-comin', pardner."

Dane roused and threw a glance down-track. Half a dozen cars, weaving, creaking, groaning, clacking as the trucks ground over the rail connection. Beyond the blinding glare of the headlamp he could just make out the dull red glow from the cab as the sweating fireman straightened from throwing on a final shovel of coal.

Dane had his anxious moment now. Suppose he had been wrong? There was no sign of the Ketchums; but should the agent be suspicious, Dane knew he would not hesitate to clear the line and slam that train on through without a stop.

The moment's strain put a jerk in his muscles, put a cold, damp sweat at the base of his neck. Then his breath eased out in a thankful sigh; the semaphore was swinging. The ruby stop light glowed and he felt the shudder of drawbars as the engineer clapped on the air. The great train slowed with a grinding squeal and the smell of locked iron on steel. And a man stepped out of the dusk — a man with a mask and a gun.

Dane couldn't be sure, but the man looked built like Jack Ketchum. The engineer must have seen him; Dane saw his hand leap for the throttle. But the masked man growled "None o' that!" and lifted his gun at the fellow. "Climb outa that cab an' be nimble! Reckon you know what I'm here for? Hop down an' make tracks!"

Kin Savvy with his mouth at Dane's ear whispered "Ketchum!" Dane nodded and with his eyes alert and narrow watched the masked man herd the engine's crew back toward the locked express car.

They were nearly there when Dane said softly: "About time we was gettin' into this, hombre."

Kin Savvy reached a hand to Dane's arm. "Not yet. I want to get that buck red-handed — an' the rest, if his gang's here with him. We'll wait till he gets his hand on the mail sacks."

"You've got about three seconds, gents," came Black Jack's voice, drifting back to them. "Better stimulate yore talkin' talents. If you can't auger that fellow into openin' the door I'm sure goin' to empty some hats out here."

Dane and Kin Savvy could hear the cab crew pleading with the stubborn express messenger. The man was still firm crouched behind his shut door when a wild-eyed figure plunged out of the brush with a shotgun grabbed to his shoulder.

The man was Jupe Dolton. He fired without a word.

Jack Ketchum staggered and the hand that held his gun let go of it, falling limply to his side. Like a flash Jack Ketchum went down on a knee. His left hand scooped up the pistol. Four quick-drummed shots spun Jupe clear around. With a gurgling scream he pitched into the brush as Dane and Kin Savvy rushed forward.

"Throw up your hands!" the Mex yelled. And his Chihuahua hat jerked back on his head to the crash of Ketchum's fired pistol.

"It sure pains me, boys," Ketchum's drawling voice said as he ducked a cool bow at the cab crew. "But I'm scared I'm goin' to have to leave you. While I'm gone you can pitch them sacks out — I'll be back in a bit an' collect 'em."

Cold as a well chain he backed from the track, ducked into the brush and was gone.

Kin Savvy fired like a maniac, emptying his six-gun completely. But it proved no kind of use, they were too far off. The hoof sound of Ketchum's flight came back to mock and deride them.

With a curse Dane turned to hunt

Dolton. They found him beside the right-of-way with his hands still clamped to the shotgun. He would never be more dead.

25

Saddle and Ride

When daylight came Kin Savvy and Dane, at the head of a posse, took up Jack Ketchum's trail. For a way it ran arrow-straight, cutting up into the hills at a speed which proved, despite his bold words, that Ketchum had no intention of returning. But after a while the hoof sign showed a diminishing speed that dropped quickly to a rambling, aimless walk; and suddenly they came upon him. He was flat on the ground, crumpled, uncaring, worn out from the loss of blood. Just the same they approached him cautiously; and it was well they did for there was fight left in him yet. He heard them coming and slithered round with his red-rimmed eyes gone slitted above the sights of a leveled pistol.

But he couldn't cut it. The pain and delirium engendered by his shattered arm, and the blood he had lost, proved too stiff a handicap. The pistol fell from his shaking hand and he fell back, mouthing curses.

Kin Savvy kicked the gun from his reach

and bent down to look at his arm. "Pretty bad shape," he muttered; and Dane said, "Might have to come off," and Ketchum swore at him blackly. Two of the posse men bound it up for him. And Kin Savvy said, "That'll have to do till we get you back to the Siding."

He squinted at Ketchum slantways. "Middle of the stream ain't no kind of place to swap horses, Jack. How come you to change your plans that way? Thought you an' Sam figured —"

"Ahr, that goddam Sam! How was I to know the bastard would stop old Harrington on the down run? I never knowed nothin' about it till that engineer told me last night. I was goin' back to Texas an' quit the goddam game; then I happened to think it would be a good joke on the rest of 'em if I stuck 'er up single handed."

"The joke, looks like, is on you," Dane said. "But cheer up — you'll likely get your wish. You're sure goin' to quit the game, though I don't know if you'll ever make Texas."

Back at Folsom flagstop Kin Savvy dismissed the posse. And when they were alone he said, "We'll pick up Straper when we get to the Siding an' I'll telegraph Bill Reno. Bill's a special agent for this road up at Denver. He'll be wantin' to get on Sam's trail — the gang'll be into Colorado by now. Outside of my jurisdiction. I work out of Cap Leigh's office."

"What about them Rancho Grande broncs?"

Kin Savvy rasped his unshaved jaw. "I'll tell Bill to keep an eye peeled."

Dane shrugged. "What about Jackman? Goin' to let him run loose?"

"Say!" Ketchum roused from his lethargy. "You ain't lettin' Frisby skin outen this, are you?"

Dane stared; and Kin Savvy said: "Frisby? He ain't mixed in —"

"Hell he ain't! Ask Straper! It was Straper kep' me posted when them pay rolls was comin' through; an' he got the tip-off from Frisby! Frisby's in this up to his neck!"

It was nearly noon when they rode into Six-Shooter Siding. Not that noon, but the next one; and Ketchum could go no farther by saddle. Dane stayed with him while the big Mex hunted up Stroat. What Kin Savvy said to the sheriff has never been recorded; but it must have been pretty potent, for when Dane saw him Stroat was a reformed character, grave of face and uncommonly obliging.

"Have a sawbones look at Jack's arm right off," Kin Savvy told him; and as Stroat was herding the bad man off, he added: "You can forget about Jupe Dolton. He's dead an' buried at Folsom."

They left the star packer staring. "It's a toss-up where we'll find Frisby," Kin Savvy told Dane, "but we'll try the saloon first. All his section hands have quit an' he's not layin' track by himself."

They left their broncs at the hitchrack. Kin Savvy said: "You go in first — I'll come in through the back. That way, if he's there, we'll get him. An' look — don't take no chances."

Fat Hake stood behind the bar. He went utterly still when he saw Dane. Dane said: "Where at is Rail Frisby?"

The fat man stood as if a sledge had struck him. Then a nerve in his cheek started twitching.

Dane put a boot to the back-room door but the place was empty. He swung a look at big Hake toughly. Kin Savvy came in from the back. Dane said, "I guess he's drifted," and kept his gaze hard fixed on Roslem and knew when the man saw Kin Savvy's badge.

Kin Savvy said: "This is showdown, brother. If you aim to keep on peddlin' booze you better put your jaw to work. We're lookin' for Railhead Frisby."

Hake's cheeks were ashine with sweat. He swallowed twice uncomfortably. He said finally, hoarsely: "I don't —"

"Think again, an' think right this time." The Mex took the six-gun from his belt and twirled it by its trigger guard with his eyes getting brighter and brighter.

Rolsem wheezed in a panic: "They've gone to Ketchum's — him an' Jackman! They left a —"

Dane jumped for the door, cheeks ashen.

He was ripping the dust hat-high when Kin Savvy caught him, roweling his roan alongside. "Haul up, you fool! Don't go off half cocked. *Válgame Dios!*" the marshal snarled. "Slow down a bit, will you?" And he reached out to grab Dane's bridle.

But Dane swerved the bay aside, kept on with his ground-eating gallop. Kin Savvy swore. "Listen! They've only got a half-hour's start. We can catch 'em — head 'em off!"

Dane pulled in then, slowing the bay to an easy lope. Kin Savvy had his own guess when he saw the color of Dane's eyes. He said, "I wanted to pick up Straper before we went out there; but I guess he'll keep.

We swing left here — hard left, boy. Notice that wash? That'll cut us into the Logan trail above timberline. 'Less they been goin' like the hammers it'll put us between 'em and the ranch. You don't figure they'd really hurt her, do you?"

Dane said nothing, but his eyes were like chilled agate as he kneed the bay to the left. Kin Savvy eyed him uneasily. He tried to switch Dane's mind to less grim thoughts. "I've got onto why Ketchum was willin' to shoot himself out of Jupe's alibi that day we raided Rafter. Plumb scared Jupe would talk — would mebbe wire Cap Leigh what he'd seen that day he trailed 'em."

Dane kept his gaze on the trail, and his tight-clamped mouth held a curve that was wicked. Kin Savvy felt glad he was not Max Jackman.

A half-hour later they came out of the timber and turned into the Logan trail. Perhaps two miles beyond this place was the turn for Ketchum's ranch.

They pulled in their horses and Dane, bending forward, raised a cautioning hand. From below, the wind shoved horse sound up at them. There was a faint dust smell in the air; and Kin Savvy had opened his mouth to speak when abruptly the horse sound stopped. Through the mountain quiet the wind brought a smother of voices.

Telldane slipped out of the saddle and Kin Savvy's cheeks pulled taut when he saw Dane flip out his pistol and go cat-footing down the trail. With a muttered "Damn!" Kin Savvy followed. After all, perhaps Dane's way was best. Take a powerful lot of proving to pin any deadwood on Max Jackman.

There were three men in the clearing when Dane reached the brush that fringed it. Max Jackman's voice was harsh. "Put up that pistol, Luce, and let's talk this over rationally. You don't seem to understand —"

"I understand all right," Luce Jackman told them nastily. "I been expectin' somethin' like this — I've been shapin' things up for it. If you hadn't tumbled pretty quick I'd of had to figure some way of makin' you. But you *have* tumbled, an' nothing you can say can change it. You know too much. A man's first duty is to himself — you can see that, can't you? Can see that my security demands your death?"

Dane heard Kin Savvy's soft gasp behind him as Max Jackman and Frisby exchanged glances. Frisby said: "You talk like a fool, Luce." He took the pipe from his teeth and tapped its bowl on his saddle horn. "You don't suppose we'd turn you in, do you? Hell! Max's position in this country couldn't afford it: do you think they'd appoint him Governor if this stuff about you come out?"

"I guess you don't know the ol' man real well, do you, Frisby?" Luce Jackman turned his head a bit and Dane saw the feline grin that had twisted his lips. "Save your breath — whether you like it or not, your goose is cooked, same as his. There's gold on the Dolton ranch an' I've spent a heap of time plannin' how I can fall heir to it. The plans demand your death — an' you'll die. I've sweat too much riggin' up this deal, by God, to abandon it now!

"Can't you see the picture? It's simple an' cute — real cute. An' it's airtight. No shred of suspicion will be pointed my way. I been a friend to the Doltons — everyone knows it. They know, too, I been engaged to Dulcey for going on two years — leastways, they think I have; I been careful to give that impression. Another impression I've polished up, Frisby, is that you're mixed up in this thing. I've never dealt directly with Ketchum. All his dope on the pay rolls has come through Straper — that escaped lifer from Santa Fe pen. An' I've sold Straper the impression that his dope has come from Frisby; he'll be sure to have passed it on. Black Jack will swear you into the pen when they tell him he's going to hang; an' Straper can't help you out of it even if he guessed the truth. I don't take chances, Frisby: I killed Deke Straper this morning."

He laughed at their expressive faces. "Call me anything you want," he grinned. "It's all the same to me. But you ain't heard the best of this yet. I've fixed things so the Governor here will come in for his share of suspicion, too — nothing definite, of course; just a few more neat impressions. But best of all was the slick touch I added yesterday. I took out a license to marry Dulcey Dolton! So — when I finally tumbled to the truth of things, found how you two were back of all this country's troubles and learned from Rolsem that you'd ridden off toward Ketchum's ranch where that gun thrower, Telldane, an' his greaser pal left Dulcey Dolton unguarded — why, I say, what could be more natural under these circumstances than that, having found Dulcey dead on the floor —"

"You fiend!" Max Jackman shouted; and Rail Frisby said: "You've killed her?"

Luce grinned. "Not yet. We're talking now about the authorities' probable re-action when all these things are made known — I mean, what they'll think after I've had my talk with them. As I was saying: Having found Dulcey dead on the floor, and having guessed you were going there to kill her, what would be more natural than that I should temporarily go berserk, grab the law into my own hands and gun you two down like dogs?"

Luce laughed then — laughed till the tears rolled out of his eyes. Then he went on, "I don't imagine there'll be any kickback. The country will probably vote me a medal —"

"The only medal you'll get," breathed Dane, stepping out of the brush, "will be the one they bolt on your coffin!"

Like a flash Luce whirled, and flame bolted out of his gun in a livid streak — too late. Dane's gun spoke once; but Luce was dying when his finger jerked the first lead from his pistol, and his knees were already buckling when the rest kicked dust round his boots. The gun spilled from his out-splayed fist and slowly, bitterly, he followed it and lay there folded over it without sound or further movement.

Dane crossed to the dead man's father and held out his gun, butt forward. Dazedly Jackman took it, sat dully staring down at it, then with a curse hurled the thing from him and quirted his horse through the timber.

For moments the rest stood motionless. Frisby finally shook his head. "We better pack him into town," he said, not looking at Jackman's body; and Kin Savvy, nodding, strode away to get the horses.

"By grab!" Frisby muttered then, and mopped his face with his neckerchief. "We owe you a vote of thanks, Telldane. But for you we'd be where Luce is now — leastways, we'd be as dead, I reckon."

He eyed Dane searchingly: "The Rock Island's still got a place for you — got a job, I mean. Will you take it?"

Dane made no answer. Cheeks somber, he stood staring off into the trees.

"I'm talkin' at you," Frisby grunted. "I'm offerin' you a job —"

"No, thanks. I'm cuttin' loose of the gunfighter breed."

"You're —" Frisby stared. "Hell!" he said. "I'm not talkin' about *that* kind of a job —"

"I'm afraid the answer's still the same," Dane said, and stared off through the trees again to where Ketchum's ranch lay hidden.

Kin Savvy came up with the horses; took

a look at Dane and grinned. He winked at Frisby. But Frisby could not know or share the marshal's understanding of Dane's thoughts.

He said, "But I thought —"

Dane cut him off. "I'm obliged to you, Mr. Frisby, but I've got other plans."

And the light of his eyes showed wistful as he swung up into the saddle and struck off toward Ketchum's ranch.

We hope you have enjoyed this Large Print book. Other Thorndike, Wheeler or Chivers Press Large Print books are available at your library or directly from the publishers.

For more information about current and upcoming titles, please call or write, without obligation, to:

Publisher
Thorndike Press
295 Kennedy Memorial Drive
Waterville, ME   04901
Tel. (800) 223-1244

Or visit our Web site at:
www.gale.com/thorndike
www.gale.com/wheeler

OR

Chivers Large Print
published by BBC Audiobooks Ltd
St James House, The Square
Lower Bristol Road
Bath BA2 3BH
England
Tel. +44(0) 800 136919
email: bbcaudiobooks@bbc.co.uk
www.bbcaudiobooks.co.uk

All our Large Print titles are designed for easy reading, and all our books are made to last.